HATCH

The Mavericks, Book 16

Dale Mayer

HATCH: THE MAVERICKS, BOOK 16
Beverly Dale Mayer
Valley Publishing Ltd.

ISBN-13: 978-1-773365-36-7
Print Edition

Books in This Series:

Kerrick, Book 1

Griffin, Book 2

Jax, Book 3

Beau, Book 4

Asher, Book 5

Ryker, Book 6

Miles, Book 7

Nico, Book 8

Keane, Book 9

Lennox, Book 10

Gavin, Book 11

Shane, Book 12

Diesel, Book 13

Jerricho, Book 14

Killian, Book 15

Hatch, Book 16

Corbin, Book 17

Aiden, Book 18

Boxed Sets and Bundles
https://geni.us/Bundlepage

About This Book

What happens when the very men—trained to make the hard decisions—come up against the rules and regulations that hold them back from doing what needs to be done? They either stay and work within the constraints given to them or they walk away. Only now, for a select few, they have another option:

The Mavericks. A covert black ops team that steps up and break all the rules … but gets the job done.

Welcome to a new military romance series by *USA Today* best-selling author Dale Mayer. A series where you meet new friends and just might get to meet old ones too in this raw and compelling look at the men who keep us safe every day from the darkness where they operate—and live—in the shadows … until someone special helps them step into the light.

Hatch is more than happy to step up and to rescue the missing father-and-daughter archeological duo. Now if only it were that easy. They'd been questioned by the Egyptian government and released, with a warning to not leave Cairo. But, when their hotel room is found empty, most believe they took off ahead of punishment—but not Hatch's team.

When the father's foreman turns up dead, Hatch investigates the body-dump location and finds the daughter, weaving through the sand, ready to collapse.

Milly is shaken and grieving. During her captivity, her father dies, and she escapes, only to find herself lost in the sand dunes. She may be safe, but her father will never come home. Millie is determined to find the man responsible for her father's death and for the information that's changed her entire life.

Sign up to be notified of all Dale's releases here!

https://geni.us/DaleNews

PROLOGUE

H ATCH COLLAR HAD convalesced on the California base, per Mavericks' orders. He stretched out his legs and gave his arms and shoulders a good shake. It had been two weeks since the end of the last mission, and his body was back in fighting form again. And that was a damn good thing because he was raring and ready to go. Killian and Stacey had gone away for a week, and now they were back, only a couple blocks away. They were happily rearranging their lives, as they figured out what they would do.

Hatch wished them well, and what she had said—that Hatch's time for a true relationship would come—kept ringing in the back of his head.

The Mavericks had a bit of a running joke going on the subject. And, while nobody could do anything to force a *happily ever after* ending, Hatch really hoped that one day, maybe, if he were lucky enough, he'd find the right person too.

The phone rang, and he snatched it up and saw it was Killian. "What's the matter? You bored with your time off already?" he teased.

"Well, the time off was last week," he noted. "Back to work now." A serious note was in his voice.

"Oh, what's up?" Hatch asked.

"An archaeologist," he said, "and his entire team."

"What about them?"

"They've disappeared out of Egypt."

"Why?"

"Well, talk from the Egyptian government said that they had been arrested for doing some illegal digging and had stolen something they had found."

"Interesting, but that's hardly what I would expect an archaeologist to do."

"Exactly, but there is also talk of somebody on his team maybe having a part in it. Anyway, they were released and subsequently disappeared."

"Great. So … what now?"

"How do you feel about Egypt?"

"I love Egypt," he replied. "Am I going?"

"You are."

"And I'm looking for an archaeologist."

"And his daughter."

"Daughter?" At that, his eyebrows shot up. "Okay."

"As of yesterday," Killian stated, "they've been officially reported as missing."

"So who's looking for them?"

"Well, they were over there on a US grant and are essentially employees of the US government. They have a very high clearance, and, now that they're missing, it's brought up some issues."

"Of course. And this isn't something they want any of the SEALs to go after or any of the other fighting teams?"

"No, they want it to be a very small, low-key investigation. In and out, quiet and fast, because they don't know whether the Egyptian government is involved somehow or not."

"Okay," he said. "That's just vague enough to keep me

guessing."

"Her name is Millie—short for Millicent—Bragner. Her father is Marcus Bragner."

"*Oh*." Hatch whistled. "I've been to one of her speaking events. However, he's the one who's been a strong protester against the current Egyptian government."

"Right, which just adds to it. The US government has been trying to keep the peace, and Marcus has been causing quite a ruckus. When he was arrested, the US stepped in to try to smooth out the issues. Then he was released, and he and his daughter promptly disappeared, so now, of course, everybody's up in arms. Including the Egyptian government, supposedly."

"Well, if they didn't have anything to do with two Americans disappearing, then of course the Egyptian government would be upset. And, if they did have something to do with it, then of course they would act alarmed because they don't want anybody to know otherwise."

"Exactly," Killian agreed. "Glad you understand. By the way, you leave in three hours."

"Gee, lots of warning, huh?"

"It's the most I could get you," he explained, "even though you're going through the base."

"Military transport?"

"All the way," he confirmed.

"Okay, I'll be there."

"I'll be your handler."

"Sounds good to me. Am I getting a partner?"

"You are." He laughed. "And somebody who hopefully will put a smile on your face."

"I'm not such a grouch that it takes much to put a smile on my face," he protested.

"Well, you haven't seen this one for quite a while."

"Do I know him?"

"Absolutely. You used to work with him."

"Says you."

"You'll meet him at the base."

"Where?"

"On the dock. You're heading out to the destroyer. And I'm not even sure which one yet. I'll text you as soon as I hear."

"How many are in shore?"

"Three."

"That's fine," he said. "Tell my partner that I'll be there."

"Wait." There was a short moment of silence on the other end. "You're transferring to a different base because transport's already revving up to go. We initially hadn't been given clearance. But they're giving it now."

"So how quickly am I leaving?" he asked. He looked down at his gym bag. "I only have my gym bag with me."

"No problem. Your new gear bag will be in the vehicle that picks you up."

"When is that?"

"Head out now." Killian hung up.

Hatch had his wallet and his phone on him, so just walked outside.

A vehicle drove up, and a head of spiky red hair and a face filled with freckles popped out.

"Jesus. Corbin? Corbin Wallace."

"Yep, that's me." Corbin grinned.

"Great, are you my partner?"

"We've been partners forever anyway, so why not again?" he noted. "You just haven't seen me in a bit. And I must say, they patched you up pretty well, considering."

Hatch hopped into the passenger side. "Yep. So, where are we going?"

"Down to the docks and out."

"It would be nice if I had enough time to get at least one change of clothes."

"In the back, mate, in the back."

He looked in the back seat and laughed. "How damn typical."

"It so is." Corbin looked over at his buddy. "You ready to go kick some Egyptian ass?"

"I'm always ready to kick some ass. I don't think I've kicked any Egyptians lately."

"Well, we're only after the bad guys. So we have to keep an open mind if it's even Egyptians in this case."

"Too often in these cases people try to make the Egyptian government look bad. And they set it up so they look like the fall guy."

"I know," Corbin agreed.

"So what do you know about the case?" Hatch asked him.

"Only that a gorgeous chick is involved," Corbin replied. "And that means I'm on board."

Hatch laughed, shaking his head. "Well, it's my turn. If a cute chick is on board, she's mine."

"What?" Corbin asked. "How come? I'm not into having to take a number here."

"Too bad. I've waited a long time." He looked over at his buddy and grinned. "Besides, I'm better looking than you."

At that, the two of them burst out laughing. Even though it was a trip that would be fraught with danger and many twists and turns, Hatch would always be happy to have this man watch his back. Now, if only they could get to Egypt in time and find out where the family had gone— before whoever had arranged all this decided the father and daughter were more of a liability alive than dead.

CHAPTER 1

HATCH COLLAR PICKED up yet another piece of pizza out of the box in front of him and studied what was going on outside the window. "So strange." He shook his head. "You look in this direction, and everything looks like a normal busy city, but you look in that direction, and that huge pyramid just bounces out of nowhere."

"Yet for everybody here, it's normal," Corbin agreed, pyramids being normal and about what they expected to see here in Egypt. "Definitely not what anybody from the Western world expects to see."

"Yet here we are." He gave him a big smile.

Corbin looked around. "Hurry up. It's almost eleven. We need to scout the area before the heat really kicks in."

"We ain't going anywhere quickly," Hatch replied. "Besides, you know nothing here happens fast enough."

"Well, it happens faster than you think," he murmured.

"I don't know about that," Hatch countered. "Seems like everybody else here is on a different time frame when we're in a rush. They're all the slowest people in the world."

At that, Corbin laughed. "I know." He picked up a piece of pizza and bit through the tangy cheese. "This is good. A slightly different taste, but it's good."

"I know. It's an American chain, so you'd expect the same taste over here, and yet apparently just the sourcing of ingredients makes a massive difference." As he studied the piece of pizza in front of him, Hatch shook his head. "It could be a long time before we get another piece of this."

"You know what? I'm okay with that," Corbin replied. "I'd rather have gourmet food."

Hatch snorted at his friend. "Gourmet foods are fine and dandy when you can do it, but you know on these missions that we're lucky if we get any food at all."

Corbin rolled his eyes. "Hey, from what I've been hearing, you guys get fed and treated quite well in this Mavericks scenario. Better than we in the navy normally do."

"Oh, we do," Hatch replied, "but that doesn't change the fact that still, a lot of times, we're just grateful to have anything at all."

"Yeah, we've been on more than a few of those ops, haven't we?" He stared at his friend. "This is likely to be one of those missions that we wish we'd never started."

"Probably," Hatch murmured quietly. When his phone buzzed a moment later, he flicked the screen, so he could read the message. "Okay, we're good to go." At that, he snatched up one more piece out of the pizza box. "Grab that last piece. We won't let it go to waste."

"Not to mention that we don't know when the hell we'll get more."

"Exactly."

With that, the two men stood, still eating the last pieces of pizza and casually walked out the door. Hatch stopped, looked at the huge pyramid in front of him, then resolutely turned his back and walked in the opposite direction. Such a foreign thing to see right here in front of him, completely surrounded by civilization.

Not everybody got access to places like where he was

going. They were looking for a father-daughter archeology team and still had no word on their whereabouts.

So far, the Egyptian government had denied any involvement, which of course they would. It was also pretty stupid of them to get involved in something like this, when a lot of American repercussions could follow. The missing pair were American. They were in Egypt on an American grant and had the permission of the Egyptian government.

Somehow the father had gotten himself into some trouble, as he railed against the Egyptian government for what they were doing to a lot of the finds unearthed at these sites. Marcus didn't like the fact that these sites were being developed and marketed for tourists. Marcus wanted each to be kept as historical places, keeping the tourists away.

Hatch also wondered what the American government was doing by allowing somebody who let his mouth run loose come over here to begin with. Especially when Marcus's views on the Egyptian government and its interference into the archaeology sites were very well-known.

Generally the Egyptian government knew where their priorities were and took care to keep everything preserved for future generations, but, every once in a while, when things were tough, when they needed to open up something new to stay relevant in the mainstream media and to keep the tourists coming back, they did something that pissed people off.

"I still can't believe the Egyptian government let Marcus over here again," Corbin muttered.

"But it was a balancing act. Let's be realistic. Trying to keep people happy isn't easy. You can keep them happy on Friday and Saturday, but, come Sunday, they could still hate your guts. Just no keeping everybody happy all the time."

That was one of the lessons Hatch had learned a long time ago. And right now Marcus needed to keep his mouth shut. "I just hope Marcus isn't in trouble."

"That's assuming he's still alive. I know the pair a little, and trouble finds him at every turn."

"More than that, where is Millie, the daughter?" That was the worst part. … She was as opposite to her father as one could be. Hatch walked along the very busy tourist trap streets and took the first alleyway he could to get out of the heavy traffic. He looked back at his friend. "Amazing to think how many million visitors you can stuff into one country at any given time, isn't it?"

Corbin laughed. "And yet those visitors are the lifeblood for the people who live here. Those tourist dollars are everything."

"I know," Hatch replied. "Either that or the workers at the archaeology sites."

"Which is only good if you're physically fit and don't have injuries that prevent you from keeping up."

"I know, right? Hard physical labor or tourist traps? … Hard decision."

"Personally I'd take the hard physical labor each and every time," Corbin muttered. "It's not that I'm against tourists. I just don't want them in my face."

"Which means you are against tourists." Hatch laughed. "That's what everybody says. *We're not against tourists, but we don't want them in our backyard.*"

"Like any factory or dumpsite. They're not against it, and they certainly use its products and put its services to good use, but they don't want it in their backyard."

"Exactly, and you can understand that to a certain extent."

"Oh, I understand. I just don't particularly like it." He flashed his grin.

They slipped into the address for their lodgings, walking up a set of stairs, and at the top was a door. Without even hesitating, Hatch reached for the door, pushed it open, and stepped inside. Immediately the cool air surrounded them. No air-conditioning but a big lazy fan turned above his head. Hatch looked around, then nodded. "This will do nicely."

"Well, we're certainly central too."

"That's not necessarily something we want, but, until we have more information about the location of our missing Americans, no point in *not* being central. We have to be ready to run at a moment's notice."

"Got it," Corbin replied. "In other words, don't unpack."

"Go ahead and unpack." Hatch tossed his friend a bright grin. "Just be ready and make sure that whatever you need to grab is handy because that's about all the time you'll have available."

"So it'll be a two-second grab, and then we're out?"

"You got it."

Corbin looked over the place. "Two bedrooms?"

"Yep, the accommodations are usually pretty decent," Hatch noted.

"Providing they can give us any accommodations," Corbin added, with a smile.

"I'm looking forward to this." As Corbin walked through to one of the bedrooms, Hatch grabbed his laptop, sat down at the nearby table, and checked in.

Almost immediately, Killian signed on. **How was the trip?**

Perfect, Hatch replied. **This place is hot and muggy**

and overpacked as always. He got a thumbs up for that report. Hatch shook his head and quickly typed a message, asking if the Mavericks had any new intel.

Nothing helpful was the response.

"Damn." Hatch sat back, looked around, then called out to Corbin, "We'll have to start hunting without intel."

"Figured we would." He came back out in jeans and a black T-shirt. "Where do you want to start?"

"I'd say the last known location, but Millie had a couple friends she stayed in touch with. We'll start with that."

"Can you ask Killian to do it?"

"He's contacting the father's friends and acquaintances to see if Marcus gave them any idea where he and his daughter were heading or what Marcus might have been up to. I want to take a little more personal touch with Millie, getting to know her friends."

"Good enough," Corbin replied. "Do you need me for anything?"

"We need maps of the area, especially an archaeology map of what digs are currently going on. More important, we need to figure out what digs Marcus was working on recently or if he might have been working undercover." He gave Corbin a hard look.

"Anything else?"

"Neighboring towns, sinkholes, lagoons, anything of a geologic hazard."

"Right. How detailed?"

"As detailed as you can possibly get," Hatch noted. "We could be out there for a few nights."

"Got it," Corbin asked. "What about gear?"

"That's another thing. Start by putting together a list of what we'll need for ..." Hatch stopped, thought about it.

"Four to five days out in the desert."

"That'll be quite a bit."

"I know," he agreed. "Doesn't mean we're taking it all at once. We have a central location for our base, but we'll have to start traveling soon."

And, with that, Hatch pulled up the list of phone numbers of Millie's friends and took a closer look. She had two girlfriends and one male friend listed. He wondered what that last relationship was all about. Studying the name, *Strand*, Hatch shrugged and started dialing.

MILLIE BRAGNER CURLED up in the corner, her head dropped down to rest on her knees, with her arms tight around her legs, ... holding her knees against her chest. Wedged into the corner, she had no room to rock, and it was a childhood habit that she was desperate to break, but this was hardly the time.

Her kidnappers had taken her father out about an hour ago, and, so far, he'd yet to return. She lifted her head and once again stared at the dim room all around her. It was dirty, top to bottom, ... floor, ceiling, and walls. For all she knew, she was in a cave at an archeology site that she had yet to dig into herself. She was being held captive by two men for sure, possibly four.

What she knew for certain was that she'd been awake at her hotel suite when there was a knock on the door—she thought it was two nights ago—she couldn't remember anything after that. Her arm was sore, as if she'd been given a jab, or maybe somebody had used chloroform over her face and that was why she couldn't remember what happened.

Just more unanswered questions she faced along with myriad more.

Her stomach growled, and her arm hurt, and her head ached dully. So the possibilities for her injuries were almost limitless, and it sucked from start to finish. ... It all sucked. She had been angry and upset at her father and his big mouth; ... at the Egyptian government, after questioning them and releasing them; and at life in general. Her father never seemed to know when to keep his mouth shut, which had gotten him into trouble, time and time again, even though he had specifically promised her that he would keep his opinions to himself so they could have a decent time at this dig.

But, of course, he didn't keep his promise. As soon as somebody had made some comment that he disagreed with, he would go off, ranting and raving. She knew it was easy to blame the alcohol, but was that fair? As far as she was concerned, it wasn't. He was still the one who had consumed the alcohol, knowing perfectly well what it would do to him. And that, ... that just drove her mad. She almost never touched the stuff because of it.

She had just no room in her world for that kind of problem. It was embarrassing, humiliating, and downright terrifying, and she was tired of it.

They'd been picked up by the authorities several days earlier and held for questioning. When they'd finally been released, with the understanding they were not to leave town, she hadn't even been sure what to think about that. But that night at the hotel, her father had apologized to her over and over again; she hadn't forgiven him and wasn't even sure she could. She should never have come this time.

It wasn't the first time for these outbursts by her father,

and now she understood it wouldn't be the last time. No matter what he told her, no matter what lies he believed himself, it just wouldn't happen.

He was self-delusional to think he could stay off the alcohol, and she'd been delusional to think that she could believe him. And now their situation was even worse. It was one thing to have been held in a relatively humane jail cell, knowing that the Western world would be arguing on their behalf. She had wondered how long that might be, since her father had gotten the reputation as a troublemaker. If he weren't so damn brilliant at what he did, nobody would tolerate him.

But now it may not matter that he was good at what he did. Now it seemed that he'd pretty well worn out his usefulness because of the trouble he kept getting everybody into.

She raised her head once again and looked around at the room. She had already explored the area and had found absolutely no way out of it, except for the very modern door that had been bolted and shut tightly under lock and key. A new addition, she figured, in an area that probably hadn't seen the light of day for a very long time, except for these people who were using it as a hidden jail cell. And, for that, it was quite effective.

She figured at least one or two guards were on the outside; otherwise they were damn confident in their ability to keep them locked up. When she had first woken up, her stomach had been on fire, and her head had been throbbing. Both had calmed down somewhat, but then the guards came and dragged away her father. Now she couldn't do anything, except sit here, worrying about what their kidnappers could be doing to her father.

When the door opened suddenly, she stared in surprise at a stranger.

"What do you want with me?" she cried out, but her voice was raspy and raw. Probably from the drugs or from something else; she didn't know. The air was dry, dusty, and she was parched. A bottle of water was handed to her. But no answers to her question were forthcoming. "Where is my father?" Her voice gained strength after a drink.

Again no answer.

She was then handed a small packet wrapped up in cloth. She knew it was a common way for food to be moved for the locals. He definitely looked like a local, but the lack of empathy in his gaze suggested that he didn't give a crap what he looked like and that, if she didn't behave, he'd take care of her. Permanently.

She sagged back against the floor and nodded her thanks. She quickly opened the cloth, as he left, and, sure enough, it was food, some local bread. No meat but a nice soft cheese.

She ate slowly, sparing the food and water gingerly, since she didn't know when she would get more. Her guards had been decent so far, but no telling what could happen if her father became disagreeable. The jailers could withhold the bare necessities of life from her and her father and otherwise make things much more difficult. She'd heard of things like this happening before but had never been in a position where she'd been forced to experience it.

When the door opened again a while later, she looked up to see her father stumble in and fall to the ground, as the door was slammed behind him. She bolted to his side. "Poppy, are you okay?" His face was battered, and his eyes were red and teary. One was almost swollen shut.

She gasped, as she helped him to the corner where she'd been sitting, then gave him a bit of water. When he drank, she cried out, "What did they want?"

CHAPTER 2

MILLIE'S HEART ACHED, as she saw the damage to her father's face. He wasn't a fighter in a physical sense; he was a verbal fighter. Not somebody you would take into a boxing ring and punch it out with.

Her father hadn't said two words since he'd returned, but he drank the offered water slowly. When he put it down, he let his head roll back against the wall. "We are in so much trouble."

"You think? What the hell did they want?" she muttered. "And did you give it to them?"

"I can't," he replied. "They want to know the location of that tomb we heard about in the pub."

"The tomb discussed in the pub?" she repeated softly, her mind casting back. "You mean, a few nights ago?"

He nodded.

"What? This kidnapping, your beating, has nothing to do with us being picked up earlier by the Egyptian government?"

He shook his head again.

"Seriously?" She stared at him. "We don't even have a name for that tomb. We know nothing about it."

"I know. I asked him if he had any reference for me, something that would help me identify which one he was talking about, but he said that I should know that. He was sure that I had talked to somebody about it in detail at the pub ..." Her father almost choked as he coughed a bit. "His spies had told him about it, and he wanted to know before any archaeologists got there."

"Right, so he could rob it blind, I suppose," she muttered in disgust.

"Presumably," he murmured. "But I've got to tell you that he isn't your typical grave-robber type. He already has buyers lined up for anything we can get out of there."

"Ah, crap." She stared at her father. "If he's that organized ..."

"I know." Marcus nodded. "And, yeah, I got into this again, and I swore I wouldn't."

"Yeah, you did." She sat down again, still not quite ready to let her father off the hook. "I should have known better than to believe you." She sighed. "You just don't have the strength to say no to booze."

"No," he agreed, "not when I get tired and upset. Then I don't give a damn."

"Yeah? Well, getting tired and upset and not giving a damn is exactly why we're sitting here," she muttered. "And, like you said, we're in trouble."

"They'll question you too," he noted. "It's only a matter of time."

"Of course they will! And I know even less than you. I was too busy being pissed off and angry that we were in the stupid pub to begin with to pay any attention to anyone's drunken ramblings, including yours."

Marcus nodded. "I tried to tell them that, but they don't want to believe that you had nothing to do with it."

"*Great*, that'll go over really well. I'll come back looking like a punching bag too," she snapped.

He groaned. "I hope not." He paused. "If you tell them *something*, anything at all, it will go easier on you."

"Maybe so." She raised both hands in frustration. "Except I don't know anything, so we're just stuck here. Nobody even knows we're missing."

"Well, they'll know that we're missing eventually," he replied. "They just won't know where we are."

"Did you see anything about our surroundings while you were out?"

"I wasn't outside," he corrected. "I was just on the other side of this room."

"*Just great*," she muttered. "So this is a secret location, where they don't expect company or to be interrupted. Meaning, they can keep us here and randomly beat on us indefinitely."

"That's a possibility."

"I hope not, but … we never had a chance to call for help. Not a soul knows that we're … where we are. How bad is it?" she muttered.

"Well, the Egyptian government knows we're in trouble."

"Sure, but only because you didn't show up as you were supposed to, but they could easily assume we just absconded on our own. So nobody really knows differently."

He rolled his head toward her, and she saw tears in his eyes as he whispered, "You have no idea how sorry I am. I would have done anything to not have you mixed up in this."

"Damn grave robbers," she muttered. "We come up against them all the time."

"This one is different," Marcus noted. "He's organized, and he's angry."

"Why is he angry? At whom?" she asked, looking at her father.

"Because the last grave that we had found, he'd been tipped off about it but had to back off because we were already there."

"*Great*, so now he thinks we're responsible for him losing out."

Marcus nodded. "And believe me. He doesn't care how he gets paid back, but he wants the money he figures he lost out on."

"And yet, even if we did want to pay him, we don't have any to give him." She shook her head, staring at her father.

"No, we don't, and I told him that. So he wants us to find the next grave and to keep it secret, so he can have it."

"So he can plunder another rich find?" she asked in horror.

"And, of course, that's our worst nightmare, but he doesn't know that." Marcus added, "And you need to keep that in mind."

"He'll know that already. He knows far too much about us as it is. He knew where we were. He knew how to grab us, and he most certainly knew how to keep us away from everybody else."

"He knows that we're dedicated archaeologists."

"And you've been incredibly vocal regarding your opinions of the Egyptian government and grave robbers," she stated. "No way he doesn't know. So basically he's hedging his bets that he can keep us captive long enough to tell him where this next grave is, preferably one that's full of loot that he can then destroy."

He nodded. "Apparently. If it were just me, I'd tell him to *eff off,*" he murmured. "But it's not just me."

"No, and they'll use me against you." Her heart sank as she stared at her father in horror. "And, if they kill you, they've still got me to do their dirty work for them."

"I know," Marcus whispered. "We can only hope that the US government knows about this and is sending help."

"What help will they send?" she asked bitterly. "Especially after you promised them that you wouldn't cause trouble for them here in Egypt."

He winced. "We have to keep the faith. Somebody out there will care. They may not care about me, but they know you're innocent, so they'll care about you."

"Not likely." She wished he was right but knew the odds weren't in their favor. "Any care they might have had would have gone out the window with your last rampage."

He stared at her. "I'm sorry."

She relented, knowing that he meant it, at least in that moment. And the next time anything happened, he would mean it all over again. She nodded quietly. "Let's just hope that somebody in Egypt's government at least wants to get you back home again, so you can't cause more trouble here."

He snorted at that. "Even that would work, and, if you don't mind, I need to get some sleep right now." He closed his eyes and crashed.

HATCH STARED DOWN at his phone. "No, it's a serious question," he replied to the man on the other end. "They've gone missing, and I'm asking if she had any contact with you in the last twenty-four to forty-eight hours."

"No," stated Strand, a male friend of Millie's. "I haven't heard from her in months. I don't even know why you'd call me."

"Well, one of the reasons to call you was to see just how close you were," he explained, "and to see if she would call you if she were in trouble."

"Hardly," he answered. "We had one hell of a fight, and she walked out of my life. I haven't had any contact with her since."

"So, that was just before she came over here?"

"Yes, I didn't want her to go, so this is just divine," he noted bitterly.

"Interesting way to look at a woman who's now missing and possibly dead."

"Her father is a complete screwup. His life is literally just one fuckup after another," he retorted, "and so goes the lives of anybody near him. I told her not to go back there, worried that it would end badly, but she didn't want him going on his own, with nobody to look after him."

"Her father?"

"Yeah, when he gets into the booze, … man, it gets ugly, but almost always she ends up paying the price for his indiscretions."

"Interesting," Hatch noted. "What is the rest of their relationship like?"

"It's more like a mother looking after a son, instead of a father protecting his daughter," he suggested.

"How is that?"

"Ever since her mother died about ten years ago, Millie pretty well stepped into her mother's role, looking after Marcus, because, when he gets out there on a dig, he's just all about the job. He forgets to eat, forgets to change clothes. I mean, most of the time he's just a walking zombie, until he drops on the spot to grab enough sleep to carry on. So

Millie's been looking after him in that way for years. I told her that I was marrying her, not him, and that things would have to change. Of course that didn't go over well."

"No, I can't imagine it would," Hatch replied.

"Anyway, we broke it off, and I haven't had anything to do with her since. Ultimately I still think I made the best decision, although I really do miss her at times," he admitted. "She's funny. She's bright. She's superintelligent. However, she's got this very ugly blind spot when it comes to her father." And, with that, Strand hung up.

Hatch looked over at Corbin. "Interesting how families operate." Hatch then shared what little bit he'd just learned. "That's a tremendous additional strain on a daughter, looking after her basically self-destructive father. It's not as if he's defenseless, like in a coma, where he can't take daily care of himself."

"And he's probably been a drunk since his wife passed away, right?" Corbin guessed.

"How is it that the bottle is the answer for everything?"

"Not the answer. Just that temporary solution so you can forget reality sometimes."

"Oh, I get it," Hatch replied, "but this sounds like a potentially ugly scenario."

"Yeah, so she's already lost a fiancé over her father's antics, so who knows how much bitterness she's holding on to."

"Well, if and when we find them, you can ask her."

"But at least it tells us that she's single and that nobody's waiting for her. And, if anybody did their research, they would have found that out pretty easily as well," Corbin noted. "The best kind of kidnap victims are those where nobody is missing them."

"This is looking more dangerous all the time."

"Agreed."

They shared a knowing look. "We need intel as to where they were taken from," Hatch stated.

"I've got that." Corbin looked down at his notes. "Security saw them enter their rooms at ten-thirty p.m., after being released from jail. The check-in desk manager confirmed also seeing them return late that evening. After that they never left, according to the security cameras, but listen to this. There was an outage at midnight."

"Of course there was." Hatch stared at his partner without surprise. "And, gee, I guess, when housekeeping knocked the next morning, there was no answer."

"Not exactly. Marcus had had meetings with the local police and was due to report in that morning, but, when he didn't show up, the authorities entered their rooms and found their belongings still there, but the pair of archaeologists were missing."

"Well, their things being there may or may not mean anything," Hatch stated.

Corbin nodded. "The cops figured that they had just booked it. Her purse was missing, and no electronics were found."

"Sure," Hatch agreed, "but anybody could have taken that. I mean, if nothing else, you could steal them and sell them to somebody else." He pulled out his phone, called Killian on a secure line. "Any chance you can get the contents of Marcus and Millie's hotel suite gone through or an inventory of that and have it all set aside for us to pick up later?" He nodded, then disconnected.

"Anyway, the cops believe that they booked it and that they're already back in the US, so absolutely no search and rescue help for them will come from here."

"Of course not."

"Not only that, I believe they're asking for extradition."

"Wow, that seems extreme for something like causing a verbal problem for the government," Hatch replied. "It doesn't rise to the grounds for extradition, unless what he did was much worse than we know."

"Agreed." Corbin nodded. "I suspect that they'll just go through the motions because they want to make a show of force, but, at the same time, they're probably just glad to get rid of them."

"I can imagine," Hatch murmured. "Some people suck so much that simply having them out of the country is a win, and it's enough that you don't have to deal with them anymore."

"That sounds about right in this case," Corbin agreed.

"Not good for the daughter though. And, if they have disappeared, which is what our government believes, then nobody is looking for them, and that's just bad news all over again."

"Well, we're looking for them," Corbin noted.

"Sure, but it's not enough, and we both know it." Hatch raised his eyebrows and tilted his head at his partner.

"I know, but we'll find them," he replied, "and then we'll sort out the rest of it."

"What about security cameras in the streets?"

"Nope, none."

Hatch stared at him. "*Great*, a hell of a way to start."

"Not really," Corbin countered cheerfully. "The city is trying to install cameras at various locations, and they've done some upgrades, but they're pretty basic and, of course, not functioning at this point anyway. And yet ..." Corbin stopped, then shook his head. "It doesn't matter. It's the hand we've got to deal with."

"What about anybody coming or going into their hotel that night?"

"Nope. Nothing that anybody is willing to talk about anyway. However, one of the staff members didn't show up today."

"Well, that's where we start then," Hatch stated. "Was he on night shift that evening the pair went missing?"

Corbin gave him a fat smile. "Sure was."

"Good, let's go have a talk with him." Hatch frowned at Corbin. "How's your Arabic?"

"My French is great. My English is better. As for my Egyptian Arabic, well, … we have access to a translator, if we need one." He added, "I also speak Spanish."

"I do too," Hatch stated, "and Italian and, not that it'll be any help, also Icelandic."

Corbin raised his eyebrows. "When the hell did you pick up Icelandic?"

He shrugged. "I was bored for a few months, decided to add another language to my skills."

"Wow, well, you could have picked up Farsi or something useful for when doing future ops in the Middle East."

"I could have, right? But Icelandic tweaked my fancy at the time." Hatch shrugged. "Well, let's go have a talk, and hopefully this guy will speak one of the languages we know."

"If not, we call on the translator."

"Or, we can just use electronic translation," Hatch murmured.

"And maybe that too," Corbin agreed.

With that, they packed up what they needed for a quick visit and slipped out the back door of their room. "It's an interesting location here," Hatch noted and looked around.

"I know." Corbin glanced down at his arms. "The self-tanning stuff worked like a charm. No wonder the ladies use it."

Hatch nodded and looked at his much darker arms. "I spend a fair bit of time in the sun and still have a pretty good tan, but I used a little on my chest, just in case."

"Yeah, we have to blend in."

"We'll blend in a little," Hatch noted, "but mostly we'll stick out like a sore thumb."

"Not at first glance though," Corbin added.

And, with that, they headed out to the address they had for the hotel employee. They walked along the street, Hatch kept watch of their surroundings, as he went to knock at the target door. When no answer came, he looked over at Corbin. "Suggestions?"

"Hey, man, this is your show." Corbin stepped back, looking up and around.

At that, Hatch tested the handle and pushed open the door. He stuck his head in and called out, "Hey, Akra. Are you here?" Again no answer. Hatch sniffed the air but couldn't smell anything decidedly like decaying flesh. So, feeling emboldened, he stepped inside, then looked back at Corbin. "I'll be right back."

Corbin nodded, leaned against the outer wall, casually noting if anybody was watching. And, with that, Hatch slipped inside, checked the main floor, and scooted upstairs. Nobody at home. He walked back down and outside again. "Nobody's here." He stood in front of the closed front door. "At least not now."

At that, they split up and started knocking on nearby doors, talking to the neighbors. Language was a bit of a barrier, but eventually the partners met up again, after checking everyone on the block.

Hatch shared with Corbin, "Apparently he hasn't been here for several days."

At that, Corbin nodded grimly. "Yeah, that's what I got too. Doesn't sound like he'd been here all that long either."

"So, do you think he just got a new job or what?"

"Makes me wonder. That's a pretty easy job to get, I would think. He was a bellhop and just moved luggage back and forth."

"His residence doesn't line up with the pay of that low-level job very well." Hatch turned and looked at it. "There's also"—he paused as he thought about it—"not much in the way of personal belongings inside. It looked to be pretty sparse. I didn't check the kitchen."

With another look at Corbin, Hatch dashed back inside the small apartment and checked. A little bit of food was in the fridge, and some items were on the counter but no major supply of food. In the bedroom were no personal belongings at all. The bed had been slept in at some point and hadn't been made, but nothing personal was here in terms of books on the tables or pictures on the walls. Nothing to show that he'd been there long-term—or even was planning on staying.

As Hatch exited the apartment, he noted somebody on the far end of the street. "Don't look now, but, at three o'clock, we may be under observation."

"I saw him earlier," Corbin confirmed. "I suggest we split up and circle around and see if we can pin him in somewhere between us."

"Good idea." And, with that, Hatch disappeared to the left, and Corbin headed to the right. Corbin was closer, but he also knew what the guy looked like. As Hatch went around, he tried to analyze the bits of features he had caught earlier. The trouble was, with everybody wearing the heavy Egyptian robes to counter the heat, it wasn't that easy to tell people apart. Still, everybody had faint distinctions on their face and hands.

By the time Hatch caught up with a man who he thought was the guy he'd seen, Corbin walked just ten paces behind the same guy. Corbin nudged forward a bit, and Hatch nodded. He stepped right in front of the man. "Hey, we need to ask you a few questions."

The man looked at him once, then bolted directly to the left, dashing inside a store, running right through to the back. With the two men pursuing him, and the storekeeper yelling at them, both burst out on the other end, only to find an empty alley.

They looked at each other. "How far could he have gone?" Hatch asked.

They opted to split up again, and Hatch went through a couple other stores, looking for the guy, but found no sign of him. As he came around to the front of the store originally used as a detour, he apologized to the storekeeper, who wasn't mollified in the least, until money crossed hands. Then he was more than happy to have them use his back door as a way to access the alleyway. When asked if he'd seen the man before, he shook his head.

Whether he had or hadn't wasn't really the issue. The store owner wouldn't tell Hatch either way, and that would be the tale of everybody here.

Hatch and Corbin were still outsiders. No matter how well they might have blended in at first glance, they looked like tourists to a certain extent—or at least Egyptians who didn't deal with the locals. That would be yet another fine distinction for everybody here. Hatch turned to find Corbin standing here, shaking his head.

"*Great.*" Corbin shook his head. "We're off to a good start."

"And yet he's nearby somewhere."

"I know, and he's likely watching us too."

"Let's pick a spot and see if we can do a little surveillance ourselves." And, with that, they grabbed a snack and more bottled water and wandered around town, as they searched for both their stalker and the bellhop. "My best guess is our transient bellhop left the country—or at least the city. However, our stalker's not leaving and could be anywhere." Hatch sighed.

"I know," Corbin muttered. "I've been looking, but I haven't seen him."

"Yet I feel him," Hatch murmured.

"Me too, so he's here. He's just got to make a mistake."

"I suspect he doesn't make many of those."

"Which means he's a pro and is somebody we really want to talk to."

"Next time he doesn't get a chance to argue or to run," Hatch murmured. "We're still in the public streets though, and that's something we'll have to keep in mind."

Corbin nodded. "Yep. The rules and regulations and all that."

"Not only rules and regulations but the law. We're here with our government's blessings but not with the Egyptian government's permission."

"Right, an important distinction," Corbin muttered.

At that, Hatch stopped. "We're about to get company. I can feel it."

"I can't see anything yet," Corbin murmured. "How

many?"

"Two, and they don't look friendly."

"Of course not," he replied. "When do they ever look friendly?"

Hatch scrunched up the napkin in his hand and tossed it in a nearby garbage can. "Let's pick the place." Then they walked to an alleyway and quickly split apart, where Hatch came face-to-face with one man.

The stranger's hand went up to Hatch's throat and slammed Hatch against a wall.

Hatch feigned a limp posture and got out of the hold; then his right arm came up, and he reversed positions with the stranger just as fast. "If you want to talk to me," Hatch growled, his forearm pressing hard against the man's throat, "then you can ask politely at least."

The man grunted at him and struggled to kick him.

"Oh no, you don't." Hatch applied more force, while pinning the guy in place, then he continued. "I don't know why you're following us or what the hell you think you want, but I don't appreciate it." And, with that, Hatch stepped back and released him.

The man stared at him, but no give was in his gaze. "You're not wanted here. You need to get the fuck out of town."

His accent was not completely local, but it was not foreign either. "Nice accent and almost a great use of English," Hatch noted.

The man narrowed his gaze at him.

"I'm looking for someone," Hatch stated.

"Who?"

"Daughter and her father." At that, if he hadn't been watching closely, Hatch wouldn't have seen that tiny flicker in the stranger's eyes. "Right." Hatch nodded. "At least now I know that I'm on the right pathway." Hatch crossed his arms, taking one more step back to give the man enough room to try to run or to at least attack him, if he had a mind to. Hatch didn't take his eyes off his attacker to even check how Corbin was doing with his guy. But Hatch trusted his partner. They'd fought a lot of wars together.

The man shook his head. "I don't know anything about that."

"Too late," Hatch replied. "Your face doesn't lie, and it already told me exactly what I need to know. You know where they are."

"No, I don't." He casually leaned against the building. "But you guys are asking questions, and you're entering places you don't belong. You aren't one of us."

"I could never be one of you," Hatch replied, "but neither can she or her father. I want to know where they are. I want their safe release, and then we'll take them back home again."

"Not happening," the man stated bluntly.

"And why is that?"

"They know too much." He shrugged. "Besides, the government is not happy with them."

"Maybe not, but you haven't convinced me that the Egyptian government won't try to get rid of them either."

"If it isn't them, it will be somebody else. Marcus has pissed off a lot of people."

"I'm sure he has," Hatch agreed calmly. "Yet Millie hasn't."

At his use of her name, the man's eyebrows rose. They studied each other with equal measure. "This is the only warning you'll get," the stranger snapped. "Get out of town."

"Or what?"

The bigger man shoved his face forward. "Or you won't get the chance."

"Look. I just want to get Millie and Marcus out of here. Show us where they are or tell us. It would be great if you just gave us a hint in whatever direction you know they'll be," Hatch noted, "and we'll take care of the rest and just disappear."

The man laughed. "That's not happening. I don't know anything about it." But he poked Hatch in the chest. "I can tell you that a hell of a lot more people are interested in what the two American archeologists know, and it'll be way past your pay grade to get them out of here. You ain't got that kind of money, and you sure as hell don't have that kind of skill." And, with that, he turned and sauntered out of the alleyway.

After making sure that his attacker was gone, Hatch turned to look at Corbin—brushing dust off his pants as the other thug walked away too. "Did you get anything?"

Corbin looked at him in disgust. "They aren't talking."

"No, but we've certainly stirred things up," Hatch noted. "I still want to find the hotel bellhop, but that's probably a waste of time. What's your take on him?"

"I'm a little afraid that we won't ever find him," Corbin replied.

"Did you ask your thug about the missing bellhop?"

"No, but I think that's probably how they found us. Our bellhop conveniently leaves his job once we show up in town."

"It would make sense. But my guy knows about Millie and Marcus's current location—or at least knows who has them," Hatch muttered. "I saw it in his eyes."

"Doesn't mean he knows anything about why they were taken away though," Corbin replied.

"But he knew something, and he definitely knew more than he was telling," Hatch stated. "Bottom line is, Millie and Marcus are in trouble, and my guy said we didn't have the money or the skills to rescue them."

At that, Corbin whistled. "So, big money is involved, is it?"

"Well, we've got a few things here to consider," Hatch added, as they walked quietly out of the alleyway, keeping their voices low. "First, the archeologists found something, and the Egyptian government doesn't want them to make it public. Second, they found something, and another faction wants access. Third, they didn't find anything, but other parties want them to find something, and they're being held until they do."

"All of which are nebulous theories, without any proof to back them up."

Hatch shrugged. "All we know is, they were in their hotel suite, supposedly secure for the night, and, come morning, they're gone. In the hotel which supposedly had security but conveniently doesn't when it counts."

"Right, but then given this part of town—"

"The hotel was a big American chain. They should have had all the security bells and whistles. This is not exactly a part of the world considered crime free."

At that, Corbin laughed. "Is there any place in the world like that?"

"Nope, not unless you're in the middle of Canada, way up in the bush, where not many people live." Hatch chuckled.

"Sure, and then you still have predators."

"I'll take those four-legged predators over two-legged ones any day." Hatch looked around. "Even now it feels like we've got one million eyes watching us."

"And that is something to consider too," Corbin murmured. "We're working off electronic surveillance, but these locals are working off spies on the ground. Many of them. Hell, this could be a well-paid job for thousands who live here."

"Speaking of networks, if Millie and Marcus have been taken by a group who's after hidden treasure, I imagine that the antiquities network—used to move the products in and out of the country—is vast. The supply chain, the people they have, the payoffs and connections, … that must involve a massive amount of logistics. And some big dig or big treasure hunt, like this theory, would encompass dozens of people easily, if not hundreds," Hatch murmured.

They got back to their hotel and slipped up to their room. "What are the chances we were followed?"

"I don't think we were followed as much as they just know that we're here now," Corbin stated.

Hatch nodded. "Time to change rooms before we get visitors." He quickly grabbed his gear, packed his laptop, and slipped across to the door. Outside, they moved up to the top, exited on a fire escape, and looked out from the rooftop. "We can head out"—he checked his phone—"two blocks over."

"Where are you getting that from?" Corbin asked.

"Killian just sent me a new address."

"Did you tell him that we were compromised?"

"Yeah, that's the nice thing about the Mavericks. They always have an answer."

"Glad to hear it," Corbin admitted, "because we need

one. Right now actually." He nudged Hatch and pointed across to the adjacent roof, where four men raced toward them.

Hatch took one look. "Shit!" They both then bolted in the opposite direction.

CHAPTER 3

WHEN THE DOOR finally opened again, Millie lifted a weary head and stared at the man coming toward her. She'd hoped for a bottle of water, but instead she was jerked to her feet and hauled from the room. She cried out; her feet were partly numb from being in the same position for so long, and she stumbled several times. Finally she was shoved into the next room, pushed onto a chair, and handed some water. She opened the cap and drank thirstily, but, before she had her fill, the bottle was snatched away.

A very American voice said, "You shouldn't drink so much at one time."

She stared at him. "Then perhaps you should let me have more water on a regular basis."

"But then you'd just need more bathroom breaks." He shrugged. "My men have better things to do than waste time on you."

She stared at him. "If that's the case, why are we even here?" she asked bitterly, trying to see him clearly, but her eyes struggled to adjust to the lack of light.

"Your father knows something, and I need that information."

She shook her head. "If you're talking about a private dig, we don't know anything about them—only our own digs."

"Oh, I have no doubt that *you* don't." The man studied her. "However, your father is a different story. He's been out here over many, many years. He's secretive, argumentative, and he uses his ridiculous outbursts to hide what he's really up to."

She stared at him in astonishment. "Seriously? His *outbursts*, as you call them, are the result of the bottle he has buried himself in. Trust me. I should know."

The American looked at her soberly. "And I can see, as a loving daughter, that is what you believe. Nobody ever wants to see their parent in a bad light. As an archaeologist, he's one of the finest, but, as a businessman, a historian, a man who wants to preserve his treasures, ... he sucks," he stated bluntly.

Her heart sank, as she stared at him. "I have no idea what you're talking about." She didn't, and that fact was obvious on her face.

He sighed as he sat in his own chair. "Well, I believe you, ... and that's too bad."

She shook her head. "I don't even know what to say." She pinched the bridge of her nose. "Could I have some more water, please?"

The bottle was immediately returned to her. She unscrewed the cap and took a long drink, before carefully recapping it. Then the stranger took away the water bottle again. "Are you serious about your claims regarding my father?" she asked, looking at him intently.

He leaned forward. "Very serious."

"Do you have proof?"

He laughed. "I have lots of proof. But I'm not here to try to convince you of your father's betrayal."

She swallowed hard again, wishing she still had the water

bottle. "I don't want to believe it." Her voice gained in strength. "I *won't* believe it."

"You see? That's why there's absolutely no point in wasting the energy to persuade you otherwise because he's your father, and you'll believe the best that you can of him."

"This has been his life."

"Until his life went off the rails."

She stared at him. "When do you think he started doing this?"

"About ten years ago," he replied, "on the dig where your mother was murdered."

She gasped and sank back into her chair, horrified. "What?"

He nodded. "Did you not wonder what happened to her?"

"I was told," she began, denial and shock in her voice, "that she got malaria and died of the fever."

He stared at her, astonished. "Wow, it really is a daughter's love, isn't it?"

"What happened to my mother?" she cried out. Getting no response, she bolted to her feet and leaned over the table, separating her from this man. "What happened to my mother?"

"Will you even believe me?" he asked. "Because the truth, … well, let's just say, the truth's a bitch, and it hurts. You won't like it. You have your sunny little bubble around your father, but it's not based on the truth." With a nod, two men grabbed her by the shoulders and dragged her back to her chair.

She stared at him. "I need to know the truth."

"Your mother was murdered," he repeated, "on a dig. She didn't die peaceably in the night, and she didn't have a fever. A cloth was shoved over her mouth, and she was suffocated."

Millie's heart constricted in pain, and she instinctively covered it with her hands in shock.

He shook his head slowly. "You really didn't know, did you?"

She shuddered, as his words slammed into her heart. "No," she murmured, "and, by the time I got her back home again, we had no open casket or an autopsy or anything like that. … She was buried as soon as we could get it done."

"Of course," he replied, "respect for the dead and all."

Her mind just spun with this new information. Yet, at the bottom of it all, was the awareness that, if Millie had been lied to once, she could have been lied to again, … like right now. "So how do you know that's what happened?" she asked, staring at him suspiciously.

"Because one of my men killed her." She bounced to her feet again but was immediately slammed back into her chair. "Of course you're angry," he stated. "You wear your emotions on your face, you know."

Just enough amusement was in his tone to get her right back on her feet again. "You murdered my mother," she yelled, staring at him with fury.

"No," he replied immediately. "My man had instructions to bring her to me, so I could talk to her. To see if she was part of the plot to steal antiquities, along with her husband. Instead my man became overzealous, and he accidentally suffocated her. And, for that, I'm very sorry. I have since learned—or at least came to believe—that she was innocent of all wrongdoing."

Millie stared at him in shock, her heart aching at the thought of what her mother must have gone through. That and the ten years of lies. "I can't believe it," she murmured. "It's too horrible."

"Well, you need to," he said, his voice determined. "Your father never told you the truth. That should tell you something."

"Did he know?" She didn't want to believe it, but this man's statement, his assurance, her father's boozehound lifestyle—it all fit.

"Oh, he knew. He also understood that threats had been made against her life, even before that."

The blows were coming too hard and too fast, and she couldn't even react. She felt like a punching bag. She was reeling, yet maintaining her composure and an upright position on the chair—so far. It was hard for her to breathe, as she stared at this man. Finally, after a long silence, she whispered, "He knew that my mother was being threatened?"

"Well, he heard about threats against her. I don't think your mother had any idea because I don't think that he ever warned her."

And again Millie couldn't say anything. It was all she could do to formulate any response in her head. "When did you find out my mother was innocent?"

"About a year later," he said. "We knew people involved in the processing of these artifacts, and they made it very clear that she had nothing to do with any of it."

"Yet they made it clear that my father had?"

He nodded. "What we don't know is who he was doing it for—the American government, the Egyptian government, or a totally unrelated third party, some private individual or collector."

"That's impossible." She shook her head. "He never got

paid for anything."

"So, either he's a shitty businessman, or he has hidden it, where you would never see it."

"What would be the point of that?" She stared at the stranger. "The money, if there is any, … I've never seen evidence of it. He lives simply. There is no property, no holidays he enjoys, no flashy car. … There's nothing."

"But none of that matters to him, does it?" the stranger asked.

She studied the white panama hat on his head, realizing that he was far too cool, while she was dealing with the shocks of a lifetime. "No, he only believes in these digs."

"So, who do you think has funded them all this time?"

"The government," she replied, "and I do have proof of that."

"Interesting," he murmured, "while the facts underline his alternate involvement." She didn't even know what to say. "I'll leave you to think about that for a while." He stood. "You need time to process it."

She nodded slowly. "You're right. I do, and I need to talk to my father." She stared at the door, knowing her father was on the other side. As the stranger motioned to the two men, she said, "Wait. May I use the bathroom first?"

He sighed. "See? That's what happens when you have water."

"And, without water, I die," she murmured.

"I have no intention of killing you," he replied. "You're both too valuable for that to happen."

"If that is the truth," she argued, "why did you so vi-ciously beat my father? And you should have given us water and food, without me asking for it. And why drug me? I'm still sick, reeling from the effects of whatever you gave me."

"What effects?" he asked, his voice sharp.

"Headache, stomachache, cramps, sore arm," she murmured. "I don't even know if it was from something you gave me or from being carried and tossed around like a sack of potatoes."

He smiled. "Most of the time you were unconscious anyway." He waved his hand. "So it's really not a big deal."

"Not for you, giving orders to your men who are 'overzealous' and who kill people regardless of your intentions. When I wake up, completely disoriented, bruised, and sore," she muttered, "that is a big deal."

"I will see that you get something for the headache," he stated stiffly.

"Just water will do," she replied hurriedly. "Water helps the healing process."

He nodded.

"Though some food would be nice," she muttered immediately. "We must have food to live, and you know it. And the heat, … it's killing us."

"The heat is not killing you," he said affectionately. "You guys are well adjusted to the climate here."

"No," she countered immediately. "Not without water and food, we aren't."

"I'll have something sent in," he added, "and, yes, you can go to the bathroom."

With that, he again waved at the two guards, who stood at her side. When she stood again, he spoke to her. "Don't piss them off. I need you, but I don't need any trouble from you. And, if you decide to go that route," he continued, his voice taking a hard tone, "I'll just take you out and bury you for some future archaeologist to find in a dig in another three thousand years."

She stared at him, wordless, and gave a clipped nod.

Millie was jerked roughly from this room into the "bathroom" area, then given a roll of toilet paper and a small shovel. She sighed and headed off to the corner, where she was at least given a modicum of privacy. She did her business, then used the toilet paper and the sand to clean her hands, wishing for water. As she returned to her guards, the two men standing there, waiting, with sly looks on their faces, she asked, "How much water is there?"

"Not enough for your hands," one said immediately.

"Of course not," she muttered. "That would be way too hygienic."

He shrugged. "We don't have a problem."

"Yeah, well, your basic equipment is different than mine," she replied sarcastically and took better note of her surroundings, now that her eyes had adapted to the low light. One wall seemed to be part of a cliff. She didn't know where she was, but, from what she saw, the cliff appeared to be quite old. Even as she wanted to take a closer look, the men jerked her forward into the room where her father was curled up on the floor against the wall.

She raced to his side, determined to ask him questions, only to see that his sleep wasn't natural. She called out, "Poppy, wake up."

There was no answer. She looked back toward the guards at the doorway, but the door was slammed shut and locked, and she knew no help would be coming from them.

SAFE FOR THE moment in their new lodgings, Hatch quickly contacted Killian, sending him an image of the attacker he'd cornered in that alleyway earlier. **We need the rundown on this guy. He knows both Marcus and Millie, but he's not talking.**

And he's still walking? questioned Killian.

Hatch snorted at that. **Leaving bodies behind on this mission is likely to happen at some point, but, with all the eyes on us, I just didn't want to start that way so soon.**

Best if it doesn't happen at all. Egypt is not very impressed about any foreigners being there.

Hatch rolled his eyes at that. **I suppose they just want Marcus to disappear.**

Killian picked up the phone and called Hatch directly. "I'm hearing some innuendos. Something about maybe everything wasn't quite as presented."

"That would be bad news." Hatch groaned. "I suppose the American government went to bat for him."

"Many times," Killian agreed quietly. "So we need to find out exactly what's going on and preferably without egg on our face."

"I'm less concerned about the egg on the face and more concerned about making sure these two people are alive and well."

"I know. I hear you there," Killian agreed. "When you say that your tail had an idea where our people are, what did you mean?"

"That's not what I meant," Hatch interrupted. "They know these two Americans, but they aren't talking. Still, I do believe they know who has our people. All we really got was a very clear warning to get the hell out of town, before we didn't have that opportunity anymore."

"Wow, so quite a threat already, huh?"

"Yeah, which means we're already shaking up somebody's world."

"What have you done in the meantime to deserve it?"

Hatch quickly gave him a rundown of the day's events.

"Which means you're also being tracked," Killian noted thoughtfully.

"Absolutely, but what we don't know is who is behind it and what their endgame is."

"Well, their endgame is for you to stop asking questions obviously," he replied, "but the real question is, *Why?* What is it they're afraid you'll unearth?"

"No clue yet." Hatch yawned.

"Have you guys had any rest yet?"

"Not too much, plus the heat takes a bit to adapt to."

"Of course," he acknowledged. "One more thing. We have secured Marcus's and Millie's things found at their hotel. Get this. Marcus's journals were left behind. The local authorities want to catalogue everything, take photos, but I talked them into releasing everything to our third-party agent. When that's done, I'll get it delivered to you. Meanwhile, maybe lay low for the rest of the evening and do some online research. I'll send you intel on this guy as soon as I track anything down."

"The problem here," Hatch added, "is that database access won't be great, right?"

"Well, there are lots of Egyptian databases," Killian replied, "but they won't be complete. Remember. Lots of people, lots of tribes, don't really worry about recordkeeping. Some of the … more remote tribes, I guess you could call them, don't even bother coming into the cities. Therefore, they don't have paperwork. Most of them really don't want it either."

"Well, these guys appear to be running businesses of

some kind, but whether they were legit or not is a whole different story," Hatch suggested.

"Meaning, your leg breakers?"

"Yeah," he replied. "That's the impression I got."

"In which case they probably don't have any legal standing, maybe not even IDs, because, if they did, it would be pretty easy to track them down."

"I was hoping we could do it anyway." Hatch laughed.

"We'll get what we can. Talk to you in a bit." And, with that, Killian disconnected.

Hatch looked over at Corbin. "Killian's not all that confident that we'll find out much about the guys who shook us down."

"No, I'm not either," Corbin agreed. "Yet it would be interesting if we could get some idea of what's going on. I mean, if our two Americans have just gone missing, what's the point of all this cloak-and-dagger stuff?"

"Unless they went missing with some help." Hatch looked over at his friend.

"And, in that case, they didn't go willingly."

"Which I think we're pretty well agreed on, aren't we? Or do you still have doubts?"

"The problem is, we don't have any proof either way," Corbin noted seriously. "All we have, so far, is the fact that two people are missing, and nobody seems to give a crap."

"That part is what I find interesting—the fact that nobody gives a crap," Hatch stated. "When you think about it, that's really one of the biggest eye-openers here."

"Which means that the Egyptian government and the locals didn't like them," Corbin noted, with a concluding nod.

"Which is also interesting because what would be the

reasons for that?" Hatch murmured.

"One could be that they interfered in something local. Or what if they were stealing or doing something with these local artifacts that people here would consider their own."

"Well, Millie and Marcus are unearthing them, and they must have hired a lot of local people to do the grunt work, … so that makes them employers. Honestly, things are tough here these days. I would think a lot of people in this area would like to have that work."

"So, that's one thing we need to track down then. Where's Marcus's foreman? What's he doing while his boss is gone? Does he even know, or, better yet, did he have anything to do with it?" At that, Corbin leaned forward and worked away on his laptop. "I've got a name." Corbin focused on his screen, reading something. "He's also an experienced dig supervisor. Looks like he does a lot of hiring."

Hatch stretched and shrugged. "Which could just mean he knows a lot of locals."

Corbin raised his gaze from his laptop, studying his buddy for a long moment. "And what do you mean by that?"

"Both good guys and bad guys." Hatch bounded to his feet, then looked out the window. "It's dark out there, but the sun sets earlier in the summer here than we Americans are used to. Perfect time to pay him a visit."

"Always." Corbin snapped closed the laptop, then picked up his wallet. He quickly shoved it into his pocket. "Let's go."

"I presume the foreman is on watch duty."

"Yeah, possibly, but he's also gotta have somebody else to take shifts with him." Corbin held up his cell. "I've got two other names. Chances are these guys worked with Millie and Marcus pretty consistently."

"Somebody," Hatch noted, "had to be running supplies. To successfully work at any of these digs, there's got to be a whole industry here to support that dig."

"There is, and, yes, you're right. We need to talk to a few of them."

Out on the streets, the night air was a little cooler. It was still hot and muggy, but at least some of the dust had settled. Hatch looked over at Corbin. "We need some wheels."

"Already ordered," he said cheerfully, looking at his friend. "It just may not be what you're expecting." With that, he laughed and led him to another corner. There they found two dirt bikes.

"Well, that's one option," Hatch said in a pleased tone. He hopped onto the back of one, and, with Corbin on the other, they slowly drove through town, looking for the address that Corbin had up on GPS. When they pulled onto the side of the road near the intended house, they hopped off, parked their bikes, and walked around the corner to what appeared to be a front door, then knocked. This time the front door opened on its own accord, and they noted that it led to a series of other doors.

"That explains the stray number in his address," Corbin stated. "Yet it didn't make this sound like it was a series of condos."

"I don't think it's condos," Hatch suggested. "Apartments maybe."

When the door in question opened, he asked the woman standing there for the foreman. She looked at him in surprise, shook her head. "Haven't seen him today at all."

At that, Corbin made a point of looking at his watch. "When do you expect him home?"

She shrugged. "Things aren't easy for him right now," she said softly. "I thought he would have been home by now."

"When did you see him last?" Hatch stepped in closer.

She stared at him, frowning. "This morning. Why?"

He shook his head. "We're just trying to figure out where he is. We need to talk to him."

She frowned. "His boss … Everything is a mess right now." She raised her hands in frustration.

He nodded slowly. "I do understand," he murmured. "We're here trying to find his boss."

The woman stared at him, then nodded. "Yes, that would make sense." She motioned at their clothing. "You don't look like you work here."

He smiled. "No, we don't, but Millie …" he improvised, "is a friend of mine."

"The daughter?" And then, as if that confirmed something else, she nodded. "That makes sense too. She's a lovely woman."

"Can you tell us anything about Marcus and Millie?" he asked quietly.

She looked at him, bewildered. "They just left," she replied. "We all have bills to pay, but they just packed up and left." She shook her head. "I don't understand why they would do that. I am so sorry but mostly just disappointed. We can't just pack up and leave, like they did. This is our home, and people depend on this, on us." She waved her arm widely at the town.

"Listen. We don't think they packed up and left," he noted. "We think they were taken."

At that, she stopped short, her gaze going wide, as she clapped her hand over her mouth. She didn't speak.

"Do you have any idea who would do something like that?" Hatch asked.

Immediately she shook her head, but it was obvious that she wasn't aware enough to even say anything.

He waited for her to collect her wits, her mind clearly spinning. "Do you have any idea why something like that might have happened?"

Again she shook her head.

He studied her carefully but didn't see any deceit. "Now you know why we need to talk to your husband."

She nodded slowly. "I don't know where he is. I haven't seen him all day."

"If he—" Then Hatch quickly rephrased his thought. "When he comes back, could you have him give us a call?" He handed her a card.

She looked down at the name, frowned, and then nodded slowly. "Yes. I know he's looking for work. We need work in order to make some money. With this entire dig shut down, the locals are in real trouble. Likely another half-dozen digs are going on all around them, but Marcus would have paid whoever he needed to in order to keep his dig going."

Hatch nodded carefully. "If I hear anything, I'll let you know."

She looked at him, smiling gratefully. "Thank you." She backed into the house. "I appreciate that." She clutched the card in her hand, like he had thrown her a lifeline.

He stepped back, looked at Corbin, and they slowly slipped away from the house. "What are your thoughts about that?"

"I think there's a damn good chance we could be looking for a fourth missing person," Corbin murmured. "I mean, if they've already taken the next person in line of command, someone who would technically know something, it would be the foreman."

They shared a look, as they surveyed the area.

"This isn't a wealthy area," Corbin noted.

"No, but they have a place to live and steady dig work, it seems," Hatch commented. "And the wife is obviously worried, which means he would normally be home by now, and he's not."

"She's just not saying what's going on or why."

"But how can she?" Hatch murmured. "She doesn't know anything."

"And now that we've told her about the potential that Millie and Marcus were kidnapped and are being held somewhere, she has to be thinking about her own family too. Like maybe that's where her husband is or maybe that's what'll happen to her and her family if she's not quiet."

"Fear is a great intimidator."

"And not having a job or an income to raise a family on is also a huge motivator," Corbin added.

"So it's quite possible that the foreman was in on it too," Hatch stated pointedly. "But there's really no way to know at this point. And, if anybody found out, and it came back on the foreman, he would lose his job because Marcus would demand loyalty."

"Well, if you arrange to have your boss kidnapped, that typically doesn't go over so well." Corbin cracked a smile.

"No, but you and I both know what it's like to have bosses we don't like." Hatch stopped at that point, reaching their rides, and got onto his. "We should have asked her what Marcus was like as an employer," he noted.

While they were considering whether they should return

to her door again, a side door opened, and a woman slipped out. She wore a head covering, but it was obviously the same woman. Hatch and Corbin looked at each other and slid off their bikes, as she raced down the street. Following at a sedate pace, they watched as she headed into one of the shops.

Standing outside, Hatch and Corbin tried to stay hidden, as they attempted to see who all was in there. A man stood off to the side, and he and the foreman's wife got into a deep conversation, though it never went loud enough that Hatch or Corbin could hear anything. The shop itself was closed and locked. Hatch looked over at Corbin. "Ideas?"

"Well, I assume that we could just burst in there and find out the truth of what's going on," Corbin suggested, "but that's not likely to go over very well."

"Yeah," Hatch agreed. "Not likely to go over at all."

"Something is going on. … Either she's looking for assistance or she is telling somebody that we're looking for her husband."

"This guy could be a family member," Hatch pointed out, as he nodded.

"I know, and I get it. I'm not saying that she's guilty of anything. But this could be an immediate 'get the information and race out the front door' situation."

"Or, in this case, the side door," Hatch quipped.

Corbin acknowledged his comment, while they waited for the woman to be done. When she slipped back out of the shop and headed home at a hurried yet slower pace, Corbin immediately stepped up and fell in beside her. "So do you want to tell us where you just went to tell people that we were looking for Marcus and Millie?"

She gasped and stared at him in horror.

He nodded. "Yeah, we saw you. We don't want to make any trouble for you, but we really want to know who and what that was all about."

She immediately shook her head, then tried to walk faster, turning and looking around to see if anybody would help her. Thankfully the streets were deserted.

"Well, you could cry out," Hatch explained. "You could do all kinds of things, but it won't go well if you do."

Her face paled, and he shook his head.

"No, we won't hurt you," Hatch promised, "but we're serious. We're trying to find Millie and Marcus, before something bad happens to them, and I want to know what's going on here. Let's start with why you felt you had to run down there and tell this guy about us immediately." Hatch gestured toward the shop with this thumb. She started to shake, and Hatch noticed the money in her hand. "He paid you for that information, didn't he?" he murmured.

She stared at him in shock. And then her bottom lip trembled.

"You were petrified, but you didn't want to get caught with information that you hadn't handed over. Got it," Hatch said.

She stared at him. "I didn't tell you anything," she whispered. "Why would you say that?"

"It's easy enough to read what's going on in your world." Hatch gave his own headshake. "Yet it won't be helpful to us."

Back at her house again, she stepped inside, and he and Corbin followed, and she didn't like that one bit. She glanced around nervously.

"Oh, I know. You don't want me in here, and I get that," Hatch stated. "However, you have information that I need. I'll get it eventually, so you'd be better off just telling me what it is."

She shook her head and then cried out, "I can't. He told me that I shouldn't talk to anybody."

"And yet you went running up to talk to that guy in the shop."

"I didn't have a choice," she replied bitterly. "He said that I'm supposed to tell him if anything happened or if anybody came looking for my husband."

"And you don't know where your husband is?"

She shook her head. "No, and, if he doesn't come home, I don't know what I'll do."

Upstairs, he heard a baby crying. "Is that one yours?"

She nodded. "Yes, my son."

"And you're afraid that something has happened to your husband, aren't you?"

She whispered again, "Yes."

"Why didn't you tell us that before?"

She frowned. "Because I don't know you," she stated bluntly. "I don't know anything about you."

"You worked with your husband helping Marcus, didn't you?" She stared at him again, shocked at his words. "I can tell that your English is very good, so you probably helped him with supplies and running interference with the locals."

"My husband is a local," she explained. "We've lived here all our lives."

"How did you hook up with Marcus then?"

"My husband was on other digs, with other archaeologists, but Marcus snatched him away. The money was good for a while, but lately, for the past few months, he's had to take less," she murmured. "That was already hard, but we didn't know what was going on."

"Was Marcus different to you, … or did he act different recently?"

She nodded in agreement. "Yes, but again we didn't know why. We just tried to stay calm and to hope that it would all work itself out. He has a temper, you know?" she murmured.

"What did you do for him?"

She nodded. "I kept his books."

"Were there any irregularities in the accounting?" She looked at him, confused. "When you said, *you kept his books*, what did you mean?"

She motioned off to the side. "I entered all the receipts and the bills of the day. The governments, the grants, … all that had to be kept neat and tidy for them to see at any time."

"Of course," Hatch noted. "And was everything proper?"

She nodded immediately. "Yes, of course, that's the requirement. He had everything really ready, as required for inspection."

"Right." Hatch nodded. "So you read and write English as well?"

"Yes," she replied. "Many of us do. We take English in school here, and I've always worked with it somewhat."

"Okay, and what about Millie? Did you have anything to do with her?"

She shook her head. "She would bring me receipts, but her father hired me. Her father signed my paycheck." At that, she chewed her bottom lip.

"Now you're worried about getting a paycheck, aren't you?"

"Of course," she snapped. "Not much work is here. Particularly for the type of work that I do."

"Which is literally just making notations in the books?"

She nodded again and then frowned. "You seem to think that I do something else."

"No, not necessarily," Hatch replied, "but there's an awful lot more to bookkeeping than just entering some figures."

"Of course there is," she said, "but that's all he wanted me to do. He does the rest himself."

"Ah." Hatch smiled. "And do you know where he keeps all that paperwork?"

She nodded. "Yes, it's here with me."

"And may we see it?"

She immediately shook her head. "No, I can't do that. That would be a violation of everything I did for him."

"Meaning that you're supposed to keep it all private?"

"Yes, yes, of course." She shrugged. "All our suppliers, the prices we pay, … it's all in there."

"Ah, then your competitors might take some of your suppliers away. Is that it?"

She nodded. "It's a very cutthroat business," she murmured, "and the only way to make any money is to keep the margins tight."

"Of course," Hatch murmured. "But we still need to take a look at the books to make sure nothing is there that would help us find Millie and Marcus. Has anybody else seen the books?"

She shook her head. "Not yet. They are inspected once a year, sometimes twice. But, so far this calendar year, nobody has been here."

"And when was the last inspection?"

She frowned, as she thought about it. "A few months back, so it's coming up on time."

"And do you normally just hand over the books?"

She nodded. "Yes, but only to Marcus. He comes here and asks for them to ensure that the entries are up to date, and then he takes off with them."

"So you've never seen him handing them over to anybody?"

"No." She shook her head. "But what else would he do with them?"

"I don't know," he replied. "We're just trying to figure out what happened to him. So anything that happened or that is unusual, I need to know about."

She stared at him. "I don't want to think of anything happening to my husband," she whispered.

"No, of course not, and, if we find him, … believe me. We'll send him back this way. But what would have happened to them?"

"I don't know," she wailed softly. "There were always some angry people, mad about Marcus for one reason or another. I told my husband that he should get a new employer, but I got paid as well too, so he stayed with Marcus."

"Of course," Hatch agreed. "It's one thing to get another job, but it's another thing entirely for both of you to lose your income at the same time."

"I can't afford that," she said immediately. "It's not much money, but all the money helps."

Hatch nodded absentmindedly, as he thought about that.

"Who is this man you went to see?" Corbin persisted.

"He's just a local we report to." She shook her head, her voice barely above a whisper.

"Well, we'll need to go report to him too," he replied in a hard tone.

She stared at him and immediately backed up. "I can't stop you from doing that, but, if he finds out that it was me—"

"He won't know that," Corbin interrupted immediately.

Hatch added, his tone soft, "We need Marcus's ledgers." The woman's eyes rounded, and she began shaking her head nonstop. "I know that you don't want to hand them over to us. However, if we can't find Marcus or Millie or … your husband, would you turn over Marcus's books to me then?"

She gasped, one hand going to her mouth, the other to her heart.

"You wouldn't want those ledgers to get into anybody else's possession, would you?"

"No," she mumbled, looking up at Hatch. "I will give the books to you, if not to Marcus."

"Thank you," Hatch said. "Now we need to find these people, and we need a photo of your husband so we can find him."

She nodded eagerly, pulling up her phone and after picking a photo, sending it to them. "Yes, yes, please. Find them. … Send them home."

"We will." With that, Corbin and Hatch turned and walked away. Once outside, Hatch faced his partner. "Yep, we're heading straight back to the store."

"Do you even think he'll still be there?"

"No, I don't," he muttered. "He's probably gone to pass the information to somebody else."

"*Great.* One of us should have stayed behind. Maybe if we hustle, we can catch him."

When they got there, the man was just locking up and heading down the street. They quickly flanked him.

"We understand you're the person everybody reports

information to," Corbin began.

Startled, the man looked confused and pretended to not understand the language.

"That doesn't work for us," Corbin said. "We know perfectly well that you speak English."

At that, the man glared at him. "Who are you, and what do you want?"

"We're looking for Marcus and Millie," Corbin murmured. "I'm sure that your local eyes and ears have already told you that we're out here."

Hatch added, "So there is no point in lying about it."

The man shrugged, as he kept striding down the street, seemingly unconcerned at their presence. "I have no reason to lie about anything."

"So why do you pay people to let you know what's going on?"

"Because anybody in business needs to know who or what is going on in town," he explained. "Just like any city, anywhere in the world, this one has problems too. We try to contain the problems by keeping track of troublemakers."

At that, Hatch snorted. "And are we troublemakers?"

"Probably." The stranger eyed Hatch. "Whether you've caused any trouble yet or not, I don't know," he replied, "but you're here to find somebody who's disappeared. So chances are, ... you'll find more trouble than you're expecting."

"Maybe," Hatch murmured. "Maybe not."

The man stared at him and shrugged. "Your funeral."

"And I can see how you might feel that way," Corbin stated quietly, "but we're also looking for the foreman."

At that, his eyebrows shot up. "I don't know anything about that."

"Maybe not," Corbin admitted, "but somebody has to know something."

The stranger shrugged. "With the one dig shut down, and lots of bills not being paid, people are not very happy. You can bet things will get even unhappier if those bills don't get paid anytime soon."

"Who is owed money?" Hatch asked.

"The locals," the contact man said. "That's what I mean. We don't like trouble here, and having foreigners come in, set up these digs, and then not pay before they take off, … it's really bad for everybody."

"And yet you know that Millie and Marcus didn't just take off."

He looked at Hatch. "I don't know that. You can tell me that repeatedly, but I don't know that. Until I get proof, one way or the other, I'm assuming that they just took off."

"I can see why you might want to think of it that way," Hatch noted, "but what if somebody helped them take off?"

"I would expect somebody *did* help them." He stared at them as if they were fools. "Of course somebody helped them. It doesn't take much in a town like this where you can get anything you want for a little bit of money."

"I mean, what if they didn't go willingly?" Hatch asked.

At that, the other man stopped. He was big, overweight, and had a lumbering gait, so he didn't stop quickly. But, when he finally came to halt, he turned and looked at him. "If that's the case, you guys better get the hell out of town, before you're next."

"We don't scare quite so easily." Hatch glared at him. "What we need to know is who would be trying to take them out."

"I have no idea," he answered, "but Marcus made a lot

of enemies."

"Enemies here, with the locals?"

"No, not so much from the locals, but every authority around. Marcus was always arguing and scrapping and, as soon as he got any booze in him, … it just got way worse. Plenty of places here would as soon not serve him."

"But they served him anyway because he's got money."

"Exactly." The man nodded. "And everybody here needs the money."

"Of course they do."

"And, even if they didn't, they would serve him anyway because that's the industry they're in."

"Drunks aren't good for anybody," Hatch muttered. "Especially ugly ones."

"No, and I've heard that a couple times," the man said, looking at him.

"The question is, did somebody do something to fix the problem permanently?" Hatch asked him.

"I don't know," he replied. "It's possible. We get murders and muggings around here all the time. And most people knew who Marcus was because he could have such an ugly mouth on him."

"So is it possible somebody just shut him up?"

"Yes, of course it is. But do I know anything about it? No, I do not." He stopped in front of a large restaurant. "Now I'm meeting my family for an early dinner. I suggest that you disappear or continue investigating or whatever it is you think you want to do," he muttered, shaking his head. "But stay out of trouble, or you can be sure trouble will be finding you, especially if you start asking too many questions."

"Isn't that what you do?" Hatch asked him.

"No." He stared Hatch down with a hard glance. "I don't ask any questions. People come to me with information."

"Because they have no choice, I presume."

"Protection is everything in this town," he murmured. "I like to keep my friends safe. An awful lot of people here don't care so much about safety."

Hatch heard a veiled warning in that, but the threat wasn't exactly clear.

With that, the man turned and stepped into the restaurant. Hatch and Corbin stayed outside, as they watched the man being greeted, then immediately headed over to a table, where several other people were already seated.

"What do you think?" Hatch walked back down the street with Corbin.

"I think there's something rotten in Denmark," he replied. "The questions are, what it is, and just how far and how deep does that rot go?"

"Right." Hatch shook his head. "It's never easy, is it?"

"No, but it's not that hard either," Corbin replied. "What we're up against is the same thing we're up against every other time. Lies and deceit. Greed and brute force."

Hatch laughed. "So, in other words, this thing is right up our alley."

"Well, it will be if we ever get answers," Corbin noted. "We haven't been here twenty-four hours yet, and already we know that Marcus had no respect for anyone here and that the locals didn't have any for him either. They want his money, but they don't want anything to do with him."

"And yet that's not a surprise," Hatch stated. "It's essentially the same story, no matter where in the world you go, particularly where an industry is dependent on foreigners for their money. Everybody hates them but fights for a chance to serve them anyway because that's what the game is. Serve as requested and keep the money flowing, or don't and watch it dry up."

CHAPTER 4

WHEN THE FOOD and water was brought next time, Millie tried to rouse her father again but got no response. She glared at her guards. "He's unconscious." The men shrugged and didn't say anything but dropped off several bags of food, she hoped, and a bottle of water. She snatched up the water and took a small sip. She knew it wouldn't be enough water to do the job for long, but she would take whatever she could get. They weren't trying to kill her, but she had no idea what they intended for her father.

She glared down at her father. "Come on. Wake up," she muttered. Almost on cue, he moaned a bit. She rolled over, so she lay closer beside him on the cool dirt. "Wake up," she ordered, a bit more assertively.

His eyes fluttered open. "Millie?"

"Yes, it's me."

He whispered, "Did we get rescued?"

"No," she replied. "And it's been pretty rough while you've been unconscious." He opened his eyes slowly, then stared at her, and she saw the confusion in them. She winced. "How do you feel?"

"Rough. I'm getting too old for this shit."

She privately agreed but knew that, under normal circumstances, absolutely no way he would have admitted that to her. He sat up and groaned, his hands going to his head. "They beat me up pretty good, didn't they?"

"Yes," she whispered. "Here's some water." She handed him their only bottle.

He had a long sip, then handed it back to her. "What do they want?" he asked, staring at her.

"Well, maybe you should tell me that." She sat up and reached for what she hoped was food in the bags. "Are you hungry? Do you want something to eat?"

"No, my stomach is not happy."

"I wonder why," she murmured. "They worked you over pretty hard."

He nodded. "I think that's why I was out for so long."

"I'm sure it was," she murmured, but, in the back of her mind, she couldn't let go of the new information she'd gotten. "Any idea what they're after?" she asked, watching him.

He shook his head. "Something about artifacts and a dig," he murmured. "Yet not enough detail to help me figure it out. Did you talk to them?" He shuffled his body a bit, so he could lean against the wall.

She nodded. "I was hauled out there, after they brought you back."

"Did they hurt you?" He frowned at her through the dim light.

She shook her head. "No, they didn't. At least not physically. Not this time."

"That's good." Marcus sighed. "Hopefully they won't at all."

"Well, they won't as long as you give them what they want. It's the only reason they're keeping me here."

He stared at her. "What do you mean?"

"My presence is to get you to cooperate," she muttered.

"Oh." He dipped his head instead of facing his daughter.

She started eating the food that was brought, and there was quite a bit of it, which was nice for a change. She held off eating all of it and focused on just a small portion. While she ate, she studied her father. "Are you sure you don't have a clue what this is about?"

"No, I don't." He turned to her. "Why? What did they say to you?"

"Well, the man in the panama hat had quite a lot to say to me, actually. Some of it I'm really struggling with."

"Like what?" Such a challenge was in his voice that she waited a bit, just staring at him. "Well, a big one is the fact that my mother was murdered." She studied his gaze, until he slowly closed his eyes and dropped his head back. "It's true, isn't it?" she asked in disbelief.

He nodded slowly. "Yes, it's true."

"Why didn't you tell me?" she cried out.

He let his head roll over toward her. "What good would that do? She was murdered on a dig in Egypt. You had an absolute fascination for the same work that we did. She wouldn't have wanted you to lose that for fear that something like that would happen to you," he stated simply. "I knew it wasn't what she would have wanted."

"But getting murdered, my God …"

He nodded. "I know. Believe me. I know. It was just a brutal, brutal time."

"You could have told me," she snapped. "I wouldn't have held it against the country, but obviously there should have been an investigation. … There should have been something."

"There was," he began, "but, as usual, … they couldn't

find anything."

"Nothing?"

"There was no proof of anyone having murdered her," he replied. "We were on a dig. When I woke up, I went out that morning, talking with the guys, and, when I came back, she was already dead."

"I still don't believe it," she wailed. "Don't you think *that* is something a daughter should know?"

"It wasn't worth the headache and the hassle and the grief." He dropped his head into his hands, as if resting them.

"How's the head?" she whispered.

"Feels like I've been hit with a bottle over the head a few times," he noted. "It feels terrible."

"They were also asking me about some of the antiquities we have taken," she paraphrased.

"I don't know what you're talking about," he murmured, looking at her.

"They seem to think that you have been cheating. Like stealing, something along that line." She gave a wave of her hand. "It wasn't exactly clear to me, but they seem to believe that you have been filtering antiquities and artifacts out of Egypt to private collections."

He stared at her, his eyes wide. "Jesus, where are they getting that from?"

"They are quite convinced apparently," she murmured. "He's been watching you for a long time." Marcus just shook his head. "Please tell me that you're not involved in anything like that."

He turned his head and stared at her. "Did he say when this started?"

"Before Mom's death apparently. That's how he ended

up telling me that she was murdered. He assumed I already knew. Not an unreasonable assumption, considering she was my mother and all."

He shook his head, muttering, "Jesus, Jesus."

She sat here and slowly finished eating, as she watched him, then took another sip. "Do you want more water?"

"No," he snapped. "I want a drink." She motioned to the water, but he quickly made it clear. "Not that."

She winced because she was penned up with an alcoholic who didn't have any booze available. It was worse than she thought earlier, and it would make her detention here even more difficult. "I'm sorry."

"You're sorry?" He faced her. "I'm the one who got you into this situation." He paused. "I'm sorry. I can hear your mother in the back of my head right now, reaming me out for having put you in this spot."

"Well, I still don't quite know what kind of a spot it really is." She yawned; it surprised her as it broke free. "But it's certainly a spot I would like to get out of. So, if there's anything you can do to help, please give them whatever they want," she stated. "Otherwise I don't think we're getting out of here at all."

He stared at her, didn't say a word, and dropped his head onto his hands once again.

She rolled over and lay down on the dirt. It would only be harder the longer they were here. Even now, more and more questions rolled around inside her head. Irritating questions. And her father had not denied his involvement in any of this, and that worried her more than anything.

She sent out a wordless prayer to anybody who could possibly hear her, crying out for help. *Please, if somebody is out there and if somebody can give us a hand, we're desperately in need.* And, just as she went to sleep, she almost thought she heard her mother's gentle voice.

"Sleep, child. Just sleep."

The trouble with sleep was the fact that she might never wake up. And, in this scenario that her father had apparently gotten them into, that possibility was all too likely. Resolutely she closed her eyes and drifted off to sleep.

CATCHING UP KILLIAN and the rest of the Mavericks on the information Hatch and Corbin had just gathered took longer than Hatch thought it should. When he finally ran out of things to say, he looked over at Corbin. "Do you have anything to add?"

He shook his head. "Nope."

"First, your street thug is not on any known Egyptian database."

Hatch nodded. "We figured as much."

"However," Killian added, "we've ID'd the guy you just talked to and left at the restaurant," Killian stated. "He has a son, two daughters, and a wife, and, yes, he's well-known as somebody who maintains information on the place."

"And is that information for sale?"

"Yes, absolutely. He's well-known for buying and selling information. So, in other words, he has his fingers on the pulse of the city and uses it to his own advantage when the time comes."

"Exactly," Corbin agreed. "So, what has this got to do with Marcus?"

"Maybe nothing. Maybe the foreman's wife was just looking for money to put food on the table," Killian replied.

"And maybe she was right, and the information guy uses pressure to make sure that the intel is flowing in his direction. Either way, she raced to him, so that's suspicious in itself."

"Only suspicious in the sense that she already knew she could get paid for that info, but only if she got there first," Corbin added. "We utilize the same techniques to get intel ourselves … all the time."

Hatch glared at his friend. "That's not helpful."

He chuckled. "Duly noted, but, until we get an idea of where the foreman is, and if he's coming back, we need to roust out some other people on that team."

"And you have some names to go by, right?" Killian asked.

"Yes, with the help of some cash," Hatch replied, "and Corbin just pulled the addresses. We'll go make some visits."

"Just be a little quiet about it," Killian said. "The Egyptian government has asked several times if we had plans."

"I'm sure," Hatch murmured, "and, yeah, we do have plans. … We just don't have any solutions yet."

"We're getting there," Killian replied. "We'll talk soon, after you find out more from somebody." With that, Killian disconnected.

Hatch looked at Corbin, then bounced to his feet. "We missed dinner. Let's grab some food and go roust any other employees who we can find."

And that's what they did. Thirty minutes later, with their stomachs full, they approached the first address. As Hatch knocked on the door, he heard loud music inside. The door opened to reveal a young man. He stared at them, as Corbin asked for Hamum.

"Just a minute." Then he took off.

When Hamum arrived, his smile immediately fell away. "Did you find him?" he asked.

"Marcus? No." Hatch immediately knew who Hamum was asking about. "We were hoping you might have some answers."

Immediately the other man shook his head. "No. I have no answers, but all of us want to go back to work."

"Of course," Hatch agreed. "Do you have any idea if the project you were working on was considered valuable or rare or anything?"

He stared at him. "Of course it's valuable. All our work is."

"Yes, I know that," Hatch replied, "I just wondered if anything in particular about this dig may have gotten Marcus kidnapped."

"He was kidnapped?" Hamum's face paled suddenly. "I thought they just took off for some reason, and they would be back." But it was obvious from his tone that he didn't really think that at all.

"Come on. You thought that they'd taken off and *weren't* coming back, didn't you?"

He nodded slowly. "Yes, I did."

"No need for him to take off. You knew it then, and you know it still," Hatch replied.

"Except that the government was making all kinds of threats," Hamum noted quietly.

"Yes, but that's the Egyptian government." Corbin shrugged. "That's what they do. Nobody listens."

"Nobody listens, until your family is threatened," he reminded them.

"What are you saying? Did the Egyptian powers that be target or threaten Millie to get Marcus to shut up?"

"No, of course not." Hamum shook his head. "He did love his daughter."

At his use of a past-tense verb, both Corbin and Hatch sent him hard looks. "What? Is he dead?"

He stared at them in confusion. "I don't know. How would I even know that?"

"You just referred to him in the past tense, as if he were already gone."

He waved his hand. "If the government has him, he might as well be gone."

"So, is the Egyptian government something to be worried about or not?"

"Not usually, no. Unless they're on a rampage about something. Then they could make an example out of him."

"And what about another faction?" Hatch asked. "Do you know of anybody else who could have kidnapped him?"

Hamum frowned, shaking his head. "No, of course not. We were just out there, working every day, but you know it allows for us to have the rest of our lives with our families, … to put food on the table for them." Hamum stared at the two foreigners. "All we want is to keep working."

"Well, in this instance," Hatch stated, "that's not likely to happen. At least not for a while."

"So, what do I do? Should I get another job?" He shook his head. "If Marcus finds out that I have another job, I'll be fired."

Hatch frowned at that. "What do you mean?"

"Marcus wants us to stay and to work only for him," he explained. "That's nonnegotiable."

"Is there anything secretive about the work you do with Marcus?" Corbin asked.

Hamum shook his head. "No, we move dirt, day in, day

out. All we do is we move dirt. Sometimes it's easier. Sometimes it's harder, but that's all we do."

"Is there anybody else you work with who would know more?"

He stared back at them. "I don't know. Why you ask these questions?" He clearly was nervous. "Should I be worried?"

"No, I'm sure you don't need to be worried," Hatch answered in a soothing tone. "We're just trying to find Marcus."

The man started to back away. "Please don't …"

"Is there any reason why you could be in danger?"

"I'm not in danger," he said, "but people will ask questions. And the more they see me talking to you, the worse that will get." And, with that, he stepped inside and slammed the door.

"Well, that's not really a surprise though, is it?" Corbin looked at Hatch.

"No, guess not." He shook his head, as they turned and walked away. "So nobody knows anything?"

"Isn't that always the way?"

"Not like this though. They're all nervous, and they're all worried."

"Well, if Marcus is in trouble with the Egyptian government, they're probably worried that they could be in trouble by association."

"I guess that makes sense," Hatch agreed. "Yet somebody has to know something."

As they headed back toward their next address, two shadows loomed up in front of them. "You were told to leave town," one of the men said threateningly.

"Yeah, but we don't take orders really well, especially not

from thugs like you." Hatch crossed his arms over his chest, studying the two men. They looked to be the same ones they had taken on in the alleyway. "Did you guys come back for another round?"

"Very funny," the one man replied in a sour tone.

"Hey, it's not my fault," Hatch told him. "If you want to go another round, we can think about it. We just ate, so it wouldn't be a bad idea. Burn some of that off and all." He looked over at Corbin. "What about you? You ready to go another round?"

Corbin laughed. "I'm always ready for a good scrap. I'm still not sure what they think they're after though."

"We're trying to give you fair warning," the bigger man stated. "You seem to think that we're kidding."

"No, I don't think you're kidding at all," Hatch stated. "Yet you don't seem to understand that we need to get Millie and Marcus back. I mean, the Egyptian government can get involved, and we don't really care, but it won't change our position."

"It won't change ours either," the other man noted. "All the government can do is play its own games. This has got nothing to do with them."

"Well, that answered that." Hatch had absolutely no doubt that this guy was telling the truth about that. He nodded at those words. "Glad to hear that. It's one thing to deal with private issues. It's another thing when the government gets involved. They just make things messy."

The one guy snorted. "If you think this won't get messy, you don't understand this scenario very well at all."

"Oh, I think we understand it all right." Corbin smiled. "But I don't think you guys understand how committed we are to getting the answers that we need."

"You might want to change that commitment," he stated, "because we can't have you out here asking any more questions."

"Why? Because you think we're getting to the truth? Well, not so much. So far absolutely nobody is willing to offer any help. It's as if everybody wants to believe Marcus and Millie just packed up and walked away, without taking anything with them."

"They did," he agreed immediately.

"No, they sure didn't," Corbin stated. "They left too much stuff behind. Now, if you guys had at least cleaned out the hotel suite, like, … really cleaned it out, so that nothing was left, it would make more sense. But Marcus and Millie didn't have that much with them to begin with, and you even left behind some of their journals. That won't go over well."

The man looked at him, and a muscle ticked away in the corner of his mouth.

"See? Now that was something you guys didn't think of. People like us, … people like Marcus and Millie, who spend their entire lifetime hunting in these places, they don't leave their notes and their journals behind. I mean, they would literally leave their clothing and all their other possessions behind before they did that," Hatch explained. "So we know for sure that they didn't leave on their own, which means, we need to have access to them and that needs to happen now."

At that, one of the men stared at him and didn't say a word. "Any other demands?" he asked.

"You know what? We might even consider letting you guys keep Marcus, if we had some idea what the problem was," Hatch offered, "but Millie is nonnegotiable."

The man stared off in the distance. "Well, I'll pass on

the message." And, with that, the two men melted into the background.

Corbin turned and looked at his partner. "Was that wise?"

"Maybe not," Hatch said, "but we need to do something to shake things up. Nobody is talking in this damn city, and chances are that the silence will get worse before it gets better. Nobody is willing to even speculate as to where Marcus and Millie are, but these guys? … These street thugs know. There's a good chance that Millie has nothing to do with any of this. She's probably being held as collateral to make sure that her father cooperates."

"So why would they let her go?"

"It's hard to say," Hatch muttered. "Maybe her father isn't being very cooperative anyway, and maybe she's causing them more headaches. I don't know, and maybe it was a terrible idea on my part, but somehow, in the moment, it *somehow* felt right."

"That's all we have to go on sometimes," Corbin noted. "Let's hope your gut instinct was right on target here."

CHAPTER 5

WHEN SHE WOKE up again, Millie couldn't even tell what time it was because they were in complete darkness. The door opened slowly, and a guard stood there. She rolled over and sat up, searching for her father. He was here, crumpled to her side. She reached a hand over to see if he was breathing, grateful to feel it coming out slow and steady. "Thank God," she whispered.

"I presume that means he's alive," said the guard.

"Yes, he's alive."

"Good thing," he muttered. He motioned at her. "Bathroom break?"

She got to her feet, the water bottle in her hand. As she stepped out, she handed him the bottle. "Please, may I have some more water?"

He nodded. "Food is coming too."

She smiled, trying to appear pleased. "That's good news." She was operating on instinct at this point, and she wasn't particularly hungry but more concerned about keeping them both alive. So whatever effort their captors went to, she would applaud. She took several deep breaths. "It's all dark in here, so I can't tell the time of day, and my eyes miss the brightness." She shook her head. "Surely we can be held someplace where there is light."

He didn't say anything and just gave her a rough push.

"You're wasting time."

She walked around to the corner and used the *facilities,* as she mockingly referred to them, but she'd certainly used worse than that in her years on digs. She walked back toward the guard again, knowing, if she made any attempt to run, he'd come after her or just shoot her where she stood.

The fact of the matter was, out here, she had a much better chance of surviving with her kidnappers than without them. She stood in front of the guard. "May I just have a few minutes of fresh air?"

He nodded at the end of this small hallway, where the sun shone. "You can stand at the rock and wait for a minute or two, but you can't go farther than that rock."

She looked at the rock, nodded. "I'll just sit on it." She walked over, sat down, and filled her lungs with fresh air. To see the sunrise allowed her to feel some positivity in her life. More than that, she was also looking for landmarks, … trying to figure out exactly where they were.

In the distance she heard some noises, but they were too indistinct to identify them or to tell her what she heard. She closed her eyes, tilted her head up toward the sky, and whispered, "Dear God! Let this be over soon." When she heard a shout, she turned to see her guard standing nearby, calling to her.

She was only a few feet away, but he'd moved toward her father. "Is he okay?" She bolted to her feet, running to his side.

He stared down at her. "Was he alive before?"

She nodded. "Yeah! You saw me. I felt his breath on my hand."

"Sure," he noted, "but maybe there wasn't one."

She bolted inside and dropped beside her father. When

she placed her hand against his neck to check, she found no pulse. She stared down at him and gave him a hard shake. "Dad, Dad, wake up!"

But there was no response.

She looked over at her guard. "Was somebody in here?" she cried out.

He shook his head. "No, it was just … you and me."

That meant, while she had been outside enjoying the morning sunshine and fresh air, her father had been losing his life in this dark hole. The tears rolled down her face, and she dropped her head to his chest. *Dear God, Dad. What the hell is going on?*

There wasn't anything that she could do or say. There was no way to bring him back. She stared down at his features, her hand gently stroking his puffy bruised face. "You guys killed him. You know that, right?" she murmured.

"He died when nobody was here."

"It was the beating you gave him," she snapped. "He was unconscious yesterday, and now his body finally gave up the ghost." She shook her head. "He's an old man. You didn't have to beat him so badly."

At that, the guard muttered something, slammed the door in her face, and left her here beside her dead father. She closed her eyes and just held her father's hand. "Why couldn't you have told me the truth?" she whispered. "Why did you have to die now, with so many unanswered questions?"

To find out about all this deception just before he died was almost torture because she couldn't ask him about anything. Now she could never get the truth from him. She didn't know if and when he had been involved in anything. It was just pain on top of pain, and now even that was overwhelmed with the crushing grief. She closed her eyes and sobbed gently. When the door suddenly opened, she looked up and glared at the same guard, as he walked in and dropped breakfast on the ground beside her.

"What will you do with him?" she whispered, grief hitting her in waves.

"I don't know," he replied. "It's up to the boss." He turned and walked back out again.

She didn't want to eat. She didn't want to do anything but sit here and stare at her father, knowing that this was a pain that wouldn't heal quickly. Losing her father would have been terrible under any circumstances, but here and like this and with all these questions hanging over her head? It was all just too much.

If she didn't eat though, it would possibly impact her access to food in the future; plus, she knew she needed to keep her strength up. With no idea what was coming, she simply couldn't afford to let herself get weak. She needed to be as strong as possible for whatever happened next.

She just didn't know what the hell that would be. She reached for the food, and, with her dead father lying beside her, forced herself to slowly work through the process of chewing. Shaking with grief and heartache, she tried to calm herself and to focus on what she needed to do. When the door opened again about an hour later, two men walked in.

They motioned for her to get back, then picked up her father and walked out. Neither of them spoke a single word.

"What are you doing with him?" Millie ran behind them.

"It's too late to do anything for him," said the boss, standing to the side in the hallway, wearing that panama hat.

She turned to face him. "That's still doesn't answer my

question."

"He'll get buried."

"And I won't know where or when?"

"No, you won't," he stated. "Say your goodbyes now, and be done with it quickly."

She shook her head. "No, no." Tears streamed down her face, as she watched the men carry her father away. "I beg you. Don't do this," While she was crying out, her father's body was loaded onto a cart and hooked up to a motorized bike. "Is this really the way to treat the dead?"

"Look around you," he snarled. "All kinds of dead are buried here. Is this how you should be treating them?"

She stared at him in shock; then she realized he was referring to the disturbance of the dead that happened during archaeological digs. "Can I go now?" She crossed her arms over her chest. "Let me go. Please just let me take him home."

"I want to ask you something." He held up his phone. "Do you know this man?"

She stared at the image of a man. The picture was grainy. And the light too dim to see clearly. "No, I don't. Who is it?"

"He's been poking around town, asking questions about you and your father."

Immediately hope sparked inside her. "I don't know him." When the photo of a second face was held up, she shook her head. "I don't know him either. Who are they?"

"I don't know," he stated, "but they're causing trouble."

She nodded. "Not everybody would believe that we just got up and walked away. We didn't arrive anywhere, so you know somebody's bound to be looking for us."

"Well, these guys are definitely looking for you," he replied, "so there's a possibility that they might have to find you. I've got to think about this." He looked over at the men beside him. "Take her back inside. This will have to wait until I figure out what to do."

And, with that, she was ushered back into her dark enclosed grave, and the door was slammed shut behind her. The only difference was that, this time, she was all alone in this tomb. Her father, … her poor father was being dragged out to some godforsaken place in the middle of the desert, and chances were, she would never find his remains and could never give him a proper burial. And, as horrible as that was, it apparently was the least of her problems.

Who were the men looking for them? Were they potential rescuers or more enemies?

AS SOON AS Hatch and Corbin returned to their rooms, Hatch's phone rang. Not a call, a text message. He frowned at that. "Killian apparently has something to tell us." Hatch quickly acknowledged the message by calling him on a secure line. "What's up?" he asked.

"According to the scanner, a body was just found in the desert, reported as a male in his late thirties."

"Do we have an ID?"

"Not yet," he replied, "but everything fits for it to be your missing foreman."

"Ah, crap. I hope not. He's got a wife and an infant son."

"You need to find out and fast," Killian noted.

"Yeah, we're on it." Hatch disconnected. They were on the move as Hatch spoke, heading down to the police station.

"Do you really think they'll give us any help?" Corbin asked his partner.

"No, it's not likely," he admitted. "Actually I was thinking that we might do better at the morgue. At least there we might buy our way into seeing the body."

"Do we have a photo ID?" he asked.

Hatch nodded.

As it was, when they arrived at the morgue, the body was just being unloaded. They stood off to the side, waiting; one of the attendants frowned at them. Hatch held up the picture of the foreman and asked, "Is that him?"

The attendant looked at it, winced, and nodded slowly. "It's hard to confirm," he murmured.

"Why is that?"

"The heat took a toll on him."

"Of course. Any idea on how long he's been dead?" With the question, Hatch quietly slipped him a little bit of money.

The cash smoothly disappeared with a practiced movement, and the med tech shook his head. "No, we don't have that information yet. It'll be up to the pathologist to determine that."

He nodded. "But you're pretty sure it's him?"

"His ID was on the body. But, like I said, the heat has taken a toll. However, it looks like him, but I can't give you proof positive."

"Good enough." Hatch turned toward Corbin, only to see that he'd slipped into the shadows, probably already running checks to see if any reports had been filed. Hatch neared his partner. "He thinks it's him," Hatch noted, "but the body was out in the sun too long to make a positive ID at this point."

"Which would fit," Corbin replied. "He's been gone a while, I know. It's a little scary when you think about how quickly the blazing sun eats up evidence here. Tomorrow, someone will most likely do a positive ID and then contact his widow."

"We'll give her a few hours alone, before picking up Marcus's books." Hatch looked out toward the desert. "Do we have a location where the body was found?"

At that, Corbin held up his hand. "I just had it tracked and should get it back any second."

"You ready for a midnight adventure?"

Corbin nodded. "At least it's a hell of a lot cooler now. Oh, good, I've got the location." And, with that, they gassed up their dirt bikes, packed up extra water, donned their night goggles, then headed out to where the body was found. They expected to see a police perimeter or at least some official presence out here, but, when they arrived with the help of the GPS coordinates, nothing was here to find. They looked around in surprise.

"I guess in their minds they don't think any evidence is here," Corbin suggested.

"Or they've already canvassed this area and removed anything worth selling. You know there's probably not much here to find after very long in these harsh conditions."

"No, that's true." They got off their bikes and walked around the area. They saw where vehicles had turned around and where footsteps had tramped the area with complete abandon. "It doesn't appear that anybody cared much about forensic evidence either."

"The desert is pretty unforgiving. I'm guessing the standard cause of death around here is heat exhaustion and dehydration, regardless of what really happened."

Corbin nodded again, looking over at his friend. "Were you able to see the body?"

Hatch shook his head. "No, and that is a concern. I would have felt better if I could have, but the med tech wasn't alone long enough to show me."

"So, we might want to make another visit."

"Just to make sure, yes." Hatch was kicking himself for not having checked on that first.

"Ah, never mind," Corbin said. "Killian just sent a photo." He held it up, and they compared it to the one they already had of the foreman and nodded.

"Well, that's definitely him," Hatch confirmed. "But how the hell did he end up out here and why?"

They studied the area, as they searched for tracks, but found almost nothing to see. "Considering that vehicles have been all over this area, as well as far too many footprints to count," Corbin noted, "I'm presuming they've already erased any evidence that may have been here."

"Yeah, and probably without even realizing it. Wonder who called it in?" Hatch asked.

Corbin checked the preliminary report that Killian had sent. "Not much data in the report, yet says here that somebody saw the body from a distance."

"Really?" Hatch stared at him.

"They drove closer, so they ended up calling it in." Corbin turned, pointed to the road across the way. "It's possible they could have seen it from over there."

"I wonder if he was left here on purpose."

"Are we presuming he was killed here?"

"No, I wouldn't say so. He could have been dumped here, and again the evidence won't be easy to find."

"I don't think we need any evidence," Corbin noted. "I don't doubt that we have any confusion over who did it. I mean, obviously we could use some names to go along with our theory, but it'll be the same people who have taken Marcus and Millie hostage."

At that Hatch nodded. As they turned and looked around, Hatch looked at the hill behind him. "What are the chances he was thrown off the top of there?"

"Well, it would sure be nice if we saw any tracks, so we could compare to what was here—before they drove and walked all over it," Corbin snapped.

Hatch suggested, "That drop from the hill might be a possible avenue to hide the real cause of death or it certainly could be a lot easier to kill somebody that way."

"If he fell on that solid pile of rocks"—Corbin pointed—"coming down from that height, … he wouldn't have survived anyway."

Noting a spot where it looked like some of the cliff had been bashed away, Hatch said, "Look. … I think he may have hit there and come tumbling down."

"Let's go up top and take a look."

And, with that, they hopped onto their bikes, and, taking as wide a detour as needed, they made their way up to the top of the cliff. As he shut off the engine, Hatch lifted his chin. "Look. The road is over there."

At that, Corbin nodded. "Making it easy to access this hill. So quite possibly they just carried him to this point, then pitched him over."

"Alive or dead, do you think?"

"My bet is on dead," Corbin noted. "That fall alone could make it look accidental."

"Of course it could also look like he may have just flung

himself over, and they could make a good case for suicide, worried over his finances, yada, yada, especially if nobody had found the body for a long enough time. No way to prove that it was anything other than that."

Corbin sighed. "Yep."

"Hell, the killers probably made the call themselves," Hatch noted in disgust.

"That would be my take as well," Corbin murmured. "Whoever is involved in this nightmare has no intention of letting anybody walk away."

"No, and that just makes me worry even more about Millie and her father."

"Do you think they would kill Millie?"

"I think they're probably using her to make her father behave, but the problem is, what happens if and when her father refuses to cooperate? Would they take her out, or will they just focus on him?"

"What if the father isn't even around to cooperate? According to his file, he's got quite a heart condition."

"Really?" Hatch asked.

"Yeah, how did he keep up with the work?"

"Seems like that was the only thing he had."

There wasn't really any way to argue with that. "Understood."

Hatch turned and looked around, pointing off to the side. "Looks like some marks over there." They walked closer and took a look. "More tracks." He studied the area around him. It was just dark enough that it was hard to see, yet not dark enough that it would hide their own tracks. "Interesting lighting here in the desert at night."

"You feel that?" Corbin asked quietly. "I'm definitely getting the sense that we're being watched."

"I wouldn't be at all surprised. Whoever brought the body over is probably checking to see if anybody is still here."

"Yet we came up above the cliff. Do you think the police did?"

"I'm not sure they would have bothered," Hatch admitted. "Yet they could come back at another time and do an investigation. Although we also know how quickly everything disappears in the desert, whether by Mother Nature or by the greed of mankind." He knew firsthand that it happened faster than anybody would ever believe. As he studied the layout, he added, "I suspect, if we make a move in that direction, we'll end up with company."

"Good," Corbin said, "let's go then." And, with that, they casually trudged along, as if looking for tracks again. "Nobody will mistake us for cops," Corbin stated suddenly.

"Doesn't matter if they do or if they don't," Hatch murmured. "We still need to find out what happened to this guy. And yet, at the same time, these guys could lead us back to wherever the American prisoners are."

"That's what I'm hoping. If we let them make a move, maybe we'll get something we can follow," Corbin noted in a low voice. "The fact that they're even here and that they're still watching us just means that people are still very interested in this location."

"Which shouldn't come as any surprise," Hatch murmured. "If you dropped a body, … you would want to know when it got picked up, right?"

"Well, if I was stupid enough to drop a body out here," Corbin added, "I sure as hell wouldn't hang around to see if anybody was looking for evidence. You have to trust in your instincts at some point in time."

"Yeah, that's you and me," Hatch replied, with a derisive snort. "Not whoever's here."

"Well, I suggest we let them know that we're open for having a discussion."

Hatch shrugged. "The only discussion they'll want to have involves bullets."

"That would be way too noisy up here, what with how the sounds at night travel here. I suspect we're probably looking at a hand-to-hand fight. And I say, bring it on." Corbin's voice was soft but deadly serious.

At that, Hatch nodded, then raised his voice and called out, "Do you want to come down and talk to us, or are you planning on hiding, while you figure out what we're doing here? If you want to ask us questions, we'll be happy to talk."

Dead silence followed.

Hatch looked over at Corbin. "Your turn."

He looked at Hatch, then smiled, raised his voice and yelled, "Or we'll just come after you, assuming that you're the ones who killed this man."

Now came scrambling sounds in the sand nearby, and, out of the growing darkness, a bike jumped to life and took off.

Hatch and Corbin immediately raced to their bikes and followed after him.

CHAPTER 6

MILLIE WOKE UP the next morning, emotionally exhausted and heartsore. Her throat was so dry that she could hardly even breathe. She desperately needed to go to the bathroom, and she needed water. But, with nobody waking her, it felt suspiciously late, especially compared to the schedule the guards had been on previously.

And, with that thought, came the return of her worst fear. The thought that she would be left alone in here to die slowly and painfully from thirst, which had terrified her from the beginning of this kidnapping ordeal. She tried to get it out of her mind, but, once embedded, it was really hard to shake free. She didn't know what these guys wanted, but, with her father dead, no way she could even begin to provide them any semblance of what they were after.

She hoped it was all just lies, but the fact that her father was dead now meant she had no way to corroborate or to disprove the uttered words. And she desperately wanted to, and yet, at the same time, what was she supposed to say? Her father ran his business like a maverick. It was slipshod in some ways, but definitely not when it came to the forensic end of it, in terms of looking after the artifacts.

He cared about those. Now, if he cared about them because he was selling them on the private market or because he really wanted to preserve the history, she didn't know. It may well break her heart to find that out, but no doubt her father was not the same person he had been when her mother was alive.

But why would he go down this pathway? Why would he do anything to ruin his reputation when that reputation was all he had left? Stumped—and with absolutely no idea how to get the answers that she needed now that he was dead and gone—she waited in the eerie darkness for somebody to come. She wanted to scream and holler at the door, but, to preserve her parched throat, it was best for her to sit and to stay quiet.

Ultimately she could do really nothing but wait and hope that somebody would take pity on her and let her out. Finally, after what felt like another hour of dozing and sitting here, realizing her bladder situation was rather desperate, she got up, went to the door, and beat on it with her fists. When no answer came, in frustration, she reached for the door handle and pulled. And damned if the thing didn't open under her hands.

Swearing softly to herself, she pulled it open and stepped out. Judging by the faint light in the hallway, it was still night, probably a couple hours before dawn. The instinct to bolt was strong, but her need to go to the bathroom was even stronger. She quickly stepped out into the night, squatted, hating again that she had no toilet paper or anything, but she would make do because obviously any rescue of her wasn't an option at this point. She just needed to escape as quickly as she could.

Stumbling forward, she raced down the hill, hoping nobody was watching her. Out here, if somebody decided to shoot her, she could do absolutely nothing about it. Hell, even the thought of getting away free and clear wasn't much of an option at this point either.

She had no idea where she was, no idea if anybody was even out here looking for her or if she would have enough luck to stumble across somebody outside at this hour of the night or the wee morning maybe. She had no phone and no way to contact anybody. All she could do was resolutely put one foot in front of the other and keep going, hoping that she would find something.

After another ten minutes of slipping and sliding her way down the steep embankment, she heard a noise in the distance. Something like a bike. She stopped, trying to hear it again, torn between two minds, wondering whether she should call out for help, even though it could end up landing her with her kidnappers again.

Realizing she didn't have a whole lot of choice if she wanted to survive, she waited until what appeared to be the sound of the bike slowing down and then coming to a stop, and she yelled for help. She yelled over and over again, until she had to stop because her throat was too dry to keep it up.

She kept walking, feeling so tired—more than that really, … utterly exhausted, mentally, physically, and emotionally. Just as she was about to give up, she heard a sound that brought tears to her eyes. It sounded like somebody shouting for her by name. She hollered as loud as she could, but her throat was so parched that her hoarse voice cracked.

She sagged to her knees, hoping that her efforts had been enough. But, when she heard nothing, tears formed in her eyes, and she started to scream again and again. Suddenly she was picked up in somebody's arms. Immediately she fought hard, assuming it was her kidnappers. She was screaming, although it was more of a raspy shout than anything.

Finally she sagged against the strong arms in defeat. Only then she heard his voice.

"It's okay. Hey, take it easy, Millie. You need to calm down. We're here to rescue you. Easy, Millie. You're safe now. It's Hatch. Easy now."

Held against his chest, she looked up, but, in the darkness, she could barely see, but the name? … "You're here to rescue me?" she whispered. "Do I know you?"

He nodded. "Yes," he replied, as if understanding that she couldn't see much in the night. "Where's your father?"

"He's dead," she said, sobbing. "They killed him."

With his arms tightening around her, Hatch quickly led her somewhere nearby, but she couldn't even tell where that was, except for the light that suddenly flashed in her face. Caught off guard and still stunned, she finally realized that a flashlight shone into her face, and she stopped wincing against the bright light.

"We're just checking you over," the man explained. "Do you need medical attention?"

She slowly shook her head and gasped hoarsely, "Water." A bottle of water was placed in her hands, and she tilted it up and drank thirstily.

When he tried to take it away from her, she glared at him. He just smiled. "It's yours. Don't worry. You get to keep it, but remember. Too much, too fast won't be good either."

Reluctantly she slowed down on the chugging and nodded. "I know, but you don't understand how desperate you can be when you don't have water."

He still held her in his arms, and she realized that she hadn't been put down. "I can walk, you know," she stated.

He slowly lowered her until her boots touched the sand,

but almost immediately she collapsed.

She looked up at him again. "Well, I will walk. Just give me a moment."

He shook his head. "It's not necessary." Picking her up again, he asked, "Do you think you can ride on my bike?"

She looked at him and nodded. "I think so."

"Can you hold on to me?" he asked. "That's all you have to do."

She realized that he wanted to find out if she was strong enough to do that. "I can hang on," she replied, and he immediately parked her on the back of his bike. It was just a small dirt bike, and it would be a hard ride on this desert. But, as he sat down in front of her and had barely taken any of the seat, she wrapped her arms around his waist and clung to him.

If nothing else, she would hang on long enough to get out of here, hopefully back to civilization. If she was lucky, maybe she'd even get out of this nightmare. She whispered against his ear, "I don't know where my kidnappers are."

He nodded. "Hang on. Let's get the hell out of here first."

HATCH RODE AS fast as he dared, with her holding on to him, and Corbin following behind them. They were still a good twenty minutes from town. They had gone farther away from town than he had expected, while chasing after their visitor on the bike. By then they had first heard her screams. Hatch still couldn't believe it was her, but there was no doubt now. He'd seen her face and had heard her words himself.

But she wasn't in great shape. As a matter of fact, he would prefer to take her in for medical attention. She didn't seem to think that she needed it, but then he couldn't really trust that either. Realizing that her grip was struggling, he came to a slow stop. Almost like a comical scene, she slid off the bike to the ground, unconscious. He immediately parked the bike, bent to pick her up, and placed her in front of him on the bike this time. He looked over at Corbin. "She's weak, not in great shape."

"It's no wonder," he replied. "She's been through a lot. Can you ride like that?"

"I should be able to. We don't have too much farther to go."

And, with that, at a much slower pace, since he had to hold on to both her and the handlebars, Hatch drove carefully the rest of the way to the city, driving straight to their rooms. With the building in view, he parked nearby on the sidewalk, then scooped her up and headed up the rear stairs. As soon as he got her inside, he laid her on the nearest bed and lightly patted her cheeks to awaken her.

She opened her eyes and stared up at him. "What?" she whispered.

"You're in our rooms now," he explained, "but I'm a little worried about the shape you're in." It was hard to recognize the woman from a series of lectures he'd attended.

"It's just exhaustion," she murmured. "I don't even know how long I'd been walking."

He nodded. "I get that, and the fact that you're even talking is good, but—"

She shrugged. "I'll be okay. I'm just really worn out."

"That's fine, as long as I know you'll wake up," he stated. "I don't want to take a chance on you not waking up."

She stared at him for a moment and then nodded. "Got it. No need to worry. Just let me rest a bit."

"How about a shower and some food first?"

She perked up at the idea of food. "I would like both. I'm just not sure I'm strong enough." She struggled to sit up.

Hatch immediately bent down to help her. "Come on. Let's get you some food. I hate to see you crash without eating a bit first."

She looked at him. "I haven't had a whole lot of food."

"No, I get that," he murmured. "I'll be right back." He quickly made her some unbuttered toast and brewed a cup of hot tea with honey, plus a banana. When he set it before her, she stared at it for a moment, then ate in a way that showed how long she had been without proper food.

As soon as she relaxed ever-so-slightly, he said, "And here's some coffee, if you think your stomach can handle it."

She stared at him in wonder. "Coffee?"

Such reverence was in her voice that he smiled. "You can have a nap in a few minutes, but I don't want you to crash without being topped up a bit first. I'm not seeing any injuries, but are you okay?"

She nodded. "I will be. They didn't really hurt me. They beat the shit out of my father."

"Is that how he died?"

She nodded. "I think so. I have no way to know."

"Did you see him?"

"He had been badly beaten. We spoke a bit. Then he went to sleep, unconscious really. After that, he went down so fast it seemed, although being in the dark makes it hard to keep track of time. The guard came in, woke me up to let me out to use the bathroom. I checked my father before leaving the room. He was breathing but barely. I went outside for a moment, and, when the guard returned me to our room, my father was dead."

He nodded slowly. "I'm so sorry."

She nodded. "Don't get me started, otherwise I'll do nothing but cry."

"Do you know where your father's body is?"

She shook her head. "Those assholes took him. I suspect he'll end up buried in a tomb somewhere." She paused. "They even joked about leaving us for a good three thousand years for the next archaeology team to find."

He nodded slowly. "Do you know who took you?" He reached out a hand and checked her forehead.

She pulled back. "I don't know him. And I'm fine. It's nothing."

"They didn't hurt you?"

"No, and I don't know who did this." He was looking at her so intently that she hesitated before asking, "Who are you exactly?"

"You and I met years ago in England, where you were giving a series of lectures on Egypt." He smiled and pulled out his phone. "Corbin and I work for a special department of the US government."

"I'm sorry. I don't remember meeting you." She added, "I don't suppose you have any ID to that effect, do you?"

He held up his phone with his picture ID on it.

She looked at it and nodded. "So you guys are really legit? What happened to the other guy?" Then she stopped, frowned, and asked, "Or did I not see another man?"

"He's taking care of the bikes," Hatch replied calmly. "We don't want anybody following us here."

"Oh, they would have traced me already." She shook her head. "So many eyes and ears in this town that it's unbelievable."

"Yeah, we've met a few," he murmured. "Not necessarily the nicest of people either."

"No," she murmured. "I don't know who this guy was, but he was after"—she took a deep breath—"he was after some information about another site."

"Another dig site?" he asked. "An excavation?"

She nodded. "Not one I knew anything about, so, of course, I couldn't help him. And my father? ... I don't know whether he helped him or not, but they beat some things out of him—or tried to. Whatever answers he had are gone with him now, and it was that beating that ultimately killed him."

Hatch nodded slowly. "Even if it wasn't directly responsible, he wasn't in the best of shape to be out there fighting for his life."

"No," she whispered. "The one guy said a lot of awful things, and I don't know whether they were true or not." She shook her head. "I don't even want to say it out loud because, if it's true, then my faith in my father was sorely misplaced," she stated bluntly. "At the moment, I can't really even live with any of it."

"You'll have to live with all of it," he replied smoothly, "but first you need some rest. I get that you don't want to relive those experiences, but we really do need to know the full story."

She stared at him, and he watched as tears quickly pooled in her eyes. "The first thing the boss, the guy in the panama hat, told me was corroborated by my father—that my mother was murdered on a dig over a decade ago." Her voice was barely above a whisper, and, with those words, she started to cry.

He reached over, snatched her up, and held her close, as

she crumpled against his chest. "I'm sorry, not only for the kidnapping ordeal you've been through but for the loss of your father. And, with news like that, there is never a good way to find it out. I presume you didn't know about your mother?" he asked cautiously.

She shook her head, then tried to dry her tears with her hands, when he handed her a box of tissues off the bedside table. She blew her nose and settled back, not even really aware that she was still on his lap. "No, I was told that she had malaria, and, due to lack of medical facilities near the dig, she didn't survive. Nobody ever told me that she had been murdered, and that includes my father," she snapped, with bitterness. "I just don't understand. … I don't know how he could have done that."

"To protect you," Hatch replied instantly.

She pulled her head back and looked up at him. "Then you don't understand my father. He wasn't about protecting me. He was a hard man in many ways."

"But he was still your father, and undoubtedly he loved you, just like you loved him."

"I did." She paused. "And now I wonder if that love was completely misplaced."

"Let's not worry about that now," he suggested. "What else did they say?"

She slumped back against Hatch. "Some things that I tried to ask my father about, which he didn't confirm or deny, which makes it really hard."

"So your father was conscious at one point?"

She nodded. "Let me go back to the beginning."

"Let me tape this"—he shifted her onto the bed beside him—"so we don't have to go back over it too many times." He brought his phone from his pocket and pressed Record.

"Now start at the beginning.

Millie took a deep breath. "Okay. … Just a few days ago—or so it seems—we had been detained by the local authorities, questioned, then released, and were back in our hotel suite. We were already pretty upset about the accusations made by the Egyptian government and the charges they were threatening to levy. I know my father had sent out some strongly worded messages for help to the US government," she murmured, looking at him.

He nodded. "Continue."

"We were there in our rooms but decided to go get food. We were both pretty shocked, stressed, and not necessarily thinking straight," she explained. "We were trying to agree on something to eat, but we didn't get very far. The next thing I know, I was being picked up and dumped into the back of a vehicle. I did feel a jab somewhere along the line." She pointed at her arm. "But I don't know exactly when that was. Whether it was before I got into the vehicle or at the same time, it's just all a big blur."

She was lost in thought, and he had to nudge her back. "What then?"

"I did end up with quite a sore arm, and again I'm not sure whether that was from the jab or from something else, like dropping me or whatever," she muttered.

He reached out and gently stroked her arm, and then, on one of the strokes, he pulled up her shirt sleeve and studied that spot. "The injection spot could be here," he noted. "It's not obvious."

She nodded. "I didn't wake up until I was in the … cell or whatever you want to call it. It was a cave actually," she added. "Yet with a door, a modern-looking door, and a tunneled-out space was behind it, where they kept us." She shook her head. "When I woke up, my father was there, and a bottle of water was between us. We heard nothing for a very long time after that." She shuddered, just thinking about it. "I think that was the worst part, not knowing if anybody would even come back. The bottle of water made me feel like maybe they would, but I couldn't be sure."

"And when they did come back?"

"They snatched my father a while later and practically dragged him out, without saying anything. Somebody did come back a little later and gave me a little food, just bread and cheese." Suddenly her voice started to peter out. With a deep heavy sigh, she basically collapsed in his arms.

Shutting off the recorder, he immediately checked for a pulse, but she was hanging in there. It appeared that everything had finally caught up with her, and she'd crashed. He frowned at the thought and felt her forehead, just as the front door opened.

Corbin came inside, took one look at Millie, and asked, "How is she doing?"

"She just passed out." Hatch held her against his chest, happy to feel her heartbeats. "I think it's probably from exhaustion, dehydration, and stress."

"Well, she certainly has been through plenty of that," Corbin agreed quietly.

Hatch turned to put her on the bed and sat beside her for a moment. "She's pretty exhausted."

"Look what she's just been through though. How much could she tell you?"

"Quite a bit." He quickly filled in Corbin on the details.

"Wow. So her father is dead. That's not good."

"I know," Hatch murmured, "and the info sounds confusing. According to the guys who kidnapped her, her father may have known about or may have been funneling artifacts to a black market."

"Yet that doesn't fit with what we know about Marcus."

"No, but she also said that he changed ten years ago after her mother died. And that's another whole story." He then told Corbin about Millie finding out her mother had been murdered.

At that, Corbin just stared at her. "Seriously?"

Hatch nodded. "I didn't see anything in his files saying that any investigation was done."

"No, it doesn't sound like there was," Corbin replied. "Maybe I'll dig a little deeper into that." And he disappeared.

Hatch stared down at the woman sleeping soundly on the bed. "You're safe now," he murmured. He wished he had more to tell her, something that would make her feel better, but, when she woke up later, she would be stuck in this same reality. One where her father was gone and where she was potentially still in danger. Not an easy thing to tell a woman who had spent her life devoted to this work.

Then again, maybe she'd had enough. Maybe, when she woke up, she'd want to go home and would never get near another dig for the rest of her life. He doubted it though. She was one strong woman. She'd gotten away from her kidnappers on her own; whether that was by design of her kidnappers or by their sloppiness, Hatch didn't know.

But, at the moment, he was just damn grateful they had something to report and that she was here safe and sound. The trouble was, they had to make sure that she stayed that way, and that could get a whole lot more difficult going forward.

CHAPTER 7

MILLIE WOKE SUDDENLY, bolting from the bed and turning around in a circle, confused and disoriented. Almost immediately a man stepped forward, placed his hand on her shoulders. "Calm down. You're fine. You're safe."

She shrank away and stared up at him, blinking owlishly. "You." She frowned and then wavered on her feet. "Hatch?"

He immediately snatched her up and laid her back down on the bed. "Yes, me, Hatch. Before you ask, just listen. We found you wandering in the desert. We brought you back here. You've had a little bit of food, a little bit of water," he explained, "and then you collapsed again."

She stared at him. "I'm free?" she asked, shock in her voice.

"You're free."

With that came the other realization. In her mind she was free, but her father was not. Tears immediately filled her eyes. "My father is dead."

Hatch nodded and opened his arms. She threw herself in them, not sure she knew who this stranger was, but he offered something she desperately needed right now— security and comfort.

When her tears finally dried up, he settled her back on the bed. "Now take a few moments to collect yourself, and, when you're ready, food and coffee are out there."

She looked around. "Am I in a hotel?"

He nodded. "You are safe here with us. Remember. We're the good guys, so don't go tearing off, trying to escape or anything. You're not a prisoner, but we need a game plan to make sure whoever kidnapped you isn't coming after you again."

She gasped at that, her eyes huge, as she digested what he said. "You think they'll try something like that?"

"We don't know," he admitted, "because we don't necessarily understand why they came after you in the first place. So, until we have more information, we don't know whether you're safe or not. We also don't know if your escape was by design or if it was something that they weren't planning on happening."

She nodded, as memories filtered back. "I wondered that at the time." She shivered. "Any chance of a shower?"

"Absolutely. It's nine in the morning, by the way." He walked over and pulled out two towels and a washcloth. "Here you go."

She smiled as she accepted them. "Thank God. I'm really safe." She rubbed her face with her hands. She heard another voice from the other room. "Who is that?" She turned, staring at Hatch suspiciously.

At that, Corbin poked his head around the corner. "Hi. It's nice to officially meet you. I'm Corbin. I was with Hatch last night, when we found you."

Some memory retention slid back into focus, but she didn't know this other man, and his arrival had surprised her. She nodded mutely.

Hatch looked at her, smiled. "I'm Hatch. So go have a shower. You'll feel better."

And, with that, he walked out of the bedroom, leaving

her all alone. Not about to look a gift horse in the mouth, she locked the door and quickly stepped into the bathroom, locking that door as well. She wondered if she would ever get to the point where she didn't feel like she had to lock all the doors behind her.

But this wasn't the time to worry about it. She had a shower, scrubbing her head free of what seemed like weeks' worth of dust, dirt, and grime, but it had probably only been a few days. She had to admit that she didn't even have a clear time frame of her ordeal. She remembered telling Hatch several things the previous night.

Right now, it was all a big jumbled mess. She didn't know how clear or even how cognizant she had been last night—really it had been earlier in the morning. Regardless, definitely not her finest hour, but she bolstered herself with the reminder that she had gotten away, and that was what counted.

After her shower, she looked down at her discarded clothes and winced. She walked into her bedroom, toward the door, poked her head out, still wrapped up in two towels, and called out, "I don't suppose either of you have any spare clothes, do you?"

Corbin replied, "I'll go get you something. Sorry, we should have thought of that before." And, with that, he quickly walked out of the hotel suite. "We need to get your belongings brought over."

She looked at his retreating back. Hatch got up, walked over. "Don't worry. In the meantime, Corbin will find you something." Hatch went to his bag and pulled out a T-shirt and handed it to her. "For the moment though, you can wear this."

While the shirt may have been huge, as she looked at the

man in front of her, she realized that he was huge as well. "This looks like it's big enough for two or possibly three of me."

He smiled. "Good, it'll cover you to your knees then. At least the shops are open now. Corbin shouldn't be too long."

"Okay, thank you." She hesitated, looking about the suite. "Did you say there was coffee?"

He nodded.

"Let me put this on first and wrap up my hair to make sure it'll dry. Then I'll come out for coffee."

"Take your time."

She nodded and stepped back into the bathroom and yanked the towel off her head, so she could pull on the T-shirt. Then picking up the smaller towel again, she rubbed her hair to dry it off more. That was the best she could do right now, so she headed for the food and the coffee. And Hatch.

"Well, it's not exactly big enough for two of me after all." She gestured at the T-shirt. "You're no small guy either."

"Nope, I'm not," he agreed, "and neither is Corbin."

She nodded. "I'm sorry about earlier. His arrival just … startled me."

"That's fine." Hatch nodded. "I suspect for the next little while, a lot of things will startle you."

She winced. "And here I was hoping I would get over this stage faster than that."

"Don't expect too much from yourself, Millie," he noted quietly. "None of this is easy."

"No, I agree," she admitted. "I just hadn't expected it to be this hard." She sat down at the kitchenette table, wishing she had pants on, but the thought of putting on her sand-crusted pants or her underwear that she had worn for at least three days straight was enough to make her revolt.

He just nodded and handed her a cup of coffee.

She sipped it and held it close to her chest. "I shouldn't be such a coffee hog," she murmured, "but something is just so comforting about it, so normal. It reminds me of home."

He looked at her. "Copy that. Here things are very different. And yet places in the city sell an Americanized version."

"I know, but that wasn't my father's thing."

"Tell me about your father. What was he like?"

"Before my mother died or after?" she asked for clarification.

"Either. Preferably both," he replied.

"Before my mother died, my father was a man full of laughter and joy. He was the father everybody would want to have. Always ready with the hugs, always with an adventure to tell. He wanted to go places, and his motto was to live life to the fullest," she noted, with a gentle smile. "He was always on a dig, sometimes with my mother, … sometimes with me. He was rarely at home, so he was absent from my life a lot. He was this big, larger-than-life image, who would come blustering through the door, full of gifts and laughter, and it would completely change everything in my world. I think that's why I fell in love with his job because I thought that was how it would always be."

She shook her head. "And, as I grew older, while I worked with him during summer vacations and school holidays and such, it was," she murmured, "so soothing, calming, and good. But it didn't stay that way."

"No, of course not," Hatch agreed. "Reality sets in fast, doesn't it?"

"Reality, or whatever passes for reality." She shook her head. "I'm still not even sure what reality even is out here. In a way I didn't see the harsh reality of a lot of the stuff we did. I didn't handle the books. I didn't handle the staffing. He had people he'd worked with for years, so those details weren't part of my life. I just got to come to the digs and bury myself happily in the artifacts."

"Did you have anything to do with the shipping?"

"No, before my mother died, that was her thing, … and afterward he hired a company to deal with it."

"Do you know the name of that company?"

She frowned, as she thought about it. "I'm not exactly sure. It was some import-export company. I didn't really have anything to do with them."

"How long have you worked with your father?"

"Off and on for years," she replied, "but I've only been here on this particular dig with him for a few months. He wanted me to come, and I didn't really want to." She shrugged. "But, well, I came."

"Did you get the sense that he thought maybe his time with you was maybe his last time? Was there any inkling of that?"

She frowned, as she looked at him. "I don't want to think that because that would make me feel like he had some premonition about what was coming, and I don't really believe that. I think he just realized that the passage of time was happening faster than he expected and that I was already an adult and all grown up."

"Yet you didn't want to work with him?"

"Well, as it came to be, beginning after my mother's death, he wasn't the same happy-go-lucky father I'd had before," she murmured. "I don't know …" She stopped, then thought about the things that needed to be said and swallowed hard. She took a couple sips of coffee and then continued. "We had words a couple times. He was a much more difficult, a much angrier man. In fact, it was hard to be around him sometimes, and, the longer I was with him, the more I realized how much he had changed, and those changes weren't good ones. He was difficult, and certain things about him I didn't really want to accept. It had become much easier to just not be around him."

She stopped and looked at her coffee, now getting cold in her hand. "Did he miss me? Maybe." She shrugged. "I think he missed my mother terribly. I missed her too, of course, but I also lost the father I'd had before. And neither one of us could get what we wanted. Now that I think about it, it was all about Mother. She was the glue that bonded us all together."

"Your parents were really close?"

"Yes," she said, "although ... you have to understand that I spent a lot of time in boarding schools. I spent a lot of time on holidays with them, and then I was gone again. So my time with them may not have been as realistic as I assumed it was at the time. Looking back, it was likely not at all indicative of what it was like all the time."

"Right. So, in your opinion, would you say they had a good marriage?"

She nodded. "I would have said that, yes. However, I also wouldn't have thought that my father would lie to me about her death."

"Was it just too hard for him to speak of, you think? Would it just bring up so many painful memories that he thought this would be easier for him?"

She stared at Hatch. "My father wasn't emotional. He

wasn't what anyone would consider as an easygoing guy," she explained cautiously. "So I'm not really sure how to take that question. Now, if what you're getting to is asking me if he had anything to do with my mom's death, I would say absolutely not, no way. In many ways, they suited each other very well. Yet, when she had enough of his ways or his demands—because he was not easy to work with—I think she would choose another dig, then go away and work on that for a while. She had connections all over the world, and I know that better than anything. Sometimes she would just tell me that she was taking a break, and she would head down to South America."

"Is that why you went to South America?"

She winced. "You could say that." She nodded. "I wanted to be closer to my mother somehow. I never got a chance to say goodbye. I never had a chance to even understand that we were close to losing her. And it changes you. A sudden death like that? It's hard to recover from because you don't realize you even need to recover at first. And, even now, after all these years"—she sighed—"I thought I'd dealt with it, until I was in that room, talking to my kidnapper, or the one who had arranged the kidnapping."

"What did he say exactly?"

"He said something about my mother's death but spoke in a tone of voice or with a dynamic I didn't understand. He was quite surprised that I hadn't known my mother was murdered. I think he realized what a shock it was to me."

"I would imagine so," he murmured, "and, from his perspective, there was no reason for you *not* to have known."

"Maybe," she murmured, "but obviously my father didn't want me to have that information."

"Was that because he didn't want you to have that information or that he couldn't share it?"

She looked at Hatch, cocking her head.

"I guess I'm going back to the issue of emotions," Hatch added. "Is there any chance that he cared so much that he just couldn't speak about it?"

"I mean, it's possible," she replied cautiously. "All I can tell you is, … well, I got only the bare minimum of details. She was buried immediately, a graveside service for the two of us only, and that was it. It was all over and done with in a matter of days. He moved on, and I was supposed to move on too. And I felt a bitterness regarding that …" She struggled completing her sentence, and then she sighed again. "Well, as you can tell, I didn't do a very good job of dealing with it."

"When a girl loses her mother, and they are very close, … it's hard to move on," he noted gently. "Sounds like you need to spend a little bit of time and let yourself grieve her loss."

"When do I do that?" she asked, staring at him. "Because it's not just my mother now, you know? It's my father too."

"And it wouldn't be surprising if you also felt some residual anger there too," he murmured.

She stared at him. "I don't think there's *some* anger," she noted, her voice getting stronger. "I think there's *a lot* of anger. Because now? … Now I'm wondering what else he may have kept from me. I'm wondering if something he was up to resulted in my mother's death. I'm wondering if there was, … well, I can't help but wonder how much he knew about and how much he was involved in the events that brought about my mother's death."

"And this man, the kidnapper, he admitted to having a hand in your mother's death?"

"He plain and simply told me so. He said that a man who worked for him killed her. I'm not sure that the death was planned as much as maybe a case of somebody going overboard. He mentioned it himself," she murmured, thinking about it. "I don't remember his exact words, but that was the gist of it."

"Let's put your account into writing," he suggested. "Some of the other details will come to you over time."

She snorted. "And what about not allowing those details to come back because I'd be totally okay to not remember those anymore."

"That you don't want them right now is understandable," he noted, "but you will want them later, when you've got some time and distance from all this."

"Maybe," she murmured, "but it sure doesn't feel like it right now." She held out her cup. "Any chance of a second cup of coffee?"

He immediately bounded to his feet. "Absolutely. I have food for you too." He quickly loaded up a plate for her.

She stared at it. "When you're caught up in a situation like that, you're afraid you'll never get food again. Even now, I want to just move this food closer to me, in case you might want to take it away from me."

"Did they do things like that?"

"Like what?"

"Like withhold food?"

She shook her head. "No, not really. I mean, I don't want to say that they were *good* kidnappers because that just sounds so wrong," she murmured. "Honestly they had an agenda. Whether they're the ones who let me out or not, they didn't treat me terribly while I was there. They let me have water, when I asked for it, and they took me out for bathroom breaks, when I needed it." She paused. "Yet, when I wanted help for my father, … there was absolutely no help coming."

"No, but then their beef was obviously with your father," Hatch pointed out.

She nodded. "Yeah, and frankly, as far I'm concerned, my beef was with him too. I don't have him around to give me any answers anymore, and that," she noted, "is breaking my heart."

⚓

HATCH TRIED TO keep her calm and to feed her, then gave her another cup of coffee. He was waiting for Corbin to return. Hatch needed to ask her more questions about her ordeal. He wanted to make sure they understood it all a bit better. He also needed to confirm that she wasn't holding back any information. She had been kept under lock and key, and that had to make things muddy. So far, watching her eat and getting her some time to unwind seemed like a necessary step. When she finally took a break from the food, he asked, "Is that better?"

She smiled at him. "Yes, thank you. So I presume the US government sent you."

He nodded. "Yes, and, as I told you, I'm part of a special division."

She nodded. "So I presume that my father managed to get the word out."

"Well, somebody did. That is information I don't have." He shrugged. "We get orders, and we act on them."

"Of course," she replied, "and it doesn't really matter. It was just in the back of my mind, wondering how any of this came to be."

"More to the point," he continued, "let's figure out how the kidnappers knew where you were and how they decided that this was a good idea. I'd like to figure out what it was that they really wanted from your father."

"I'm not even so much concerned about that," she admitted. "All I want is to make sure that they don't think that they can come back after me again because that is definitely not what I want to deal with."

"Good point," he murmured. "So it sounds like they were looking for information on a dig."

"Right." She nodded. "And I didn't know anything about it," she immediately clarified.

"Got it. Nobody here is accusing you."

She reached up, scrubbed her face. "You're not accusing me. I get that. But I feel like I'm responsible for something here, and I don't even know what that could be."

"You're not responsible for anything," he declared. "Keep that in mind. This has been a shit show from the beginning, and you were caught up in somebody else's anger and somebody else's machinations. Let's just make sure that we get as much information as we can, so we can solve it."

"And I don't even know what it means to *solve* it now," she replied. "I just want to go home."

"What about the dig?"

"I don't even know what happened there either, but, according to the Egyptian government, I'm not allowed to continue, with or without my father," she murmured. "And, now that he's gone, I doubt I'll be allowed to continue at all."

"You were only here for a few months though, right?"

She nodded. "Yes."

"What can you tell me about your father's foreman?" he asked.

"I don't know him. My knowledge is next to nothing."

"Did you ever see him there with the kidnappers?"

She shook her head, thinking for a minute. "No, I didn't."

"You never heard his name mentioned?"

She shook her head again. "No, why would I? I don't understand what you're getting at."

"Well, he's dead," Hatch answered quietly. "We were thinking he was killed by your same kidnappers."

She stared at him in horror. "Oh my God, really?"

He nodded. "Yes, and he had a wife and an infant."

She nodded slowly. "I don't know much about his family. I just know that he and his wife were very capable. He was always there, always dealing with my father." She winced at that. "Jesus, the man deserved a big fat raise, not death."

"Was your father that difficult to deal with?"

She nodded. "Yes, and getting more so all the time." At that, Hatch raised his eyebrows, as she watched him. "Why the reaction? What difference does that make?"

"Did you ever consider that maybe he had an illness?"

She asked, "What do you mean?"

"It's just, when you said that, about him getting worse all the time, it makes me wonder. Quite a few illnesses cause mood swings. People get cantankerous, and they get more quarrelsome and more difficult to deal with as time goes on."

She stared at him. "Oh God, I really don't want to think about that."

He waited. "Meaning?"

"I don't want to think that we could have done something to help him and that I didn't see it because I was just so tired of his behavior."

"Would he have gone to get a thorough medical check-up? And if he did, would he tell you?"

She immediately shook her head. "No, he would never stand for something like that."

"In that case then, no sense in you worrying about it," he stated. "I get that it's too late to do anything about it now, and that won't be an answer that you want to live with, but it is the truth." Bitter laughter erupted from her mouth, and he immediately reached across and grabbed her hand. "Stop it now. You have to stop beating yourself up." He watched her expression as it changed. "I get it. You're stressed out over all this. Too many blows all at once. But right now you need to begin to heal, and we need to make sure that you're safe."

"That means, … I need to go home." She scrubbed the tears from her face.

"What about back to South America?"

She stared at him and then shrugged. "I don't even know what to say about that. I can't just walk onto a dig and start a new job. I'd have to have an invitation, and I don't have that right now. I think, at the moment, I need to deal with my family scenario first. Then reconsider my future and what I want then."

"Did your father leave a mess in terms of his estate?"

"No, not really. He had some things that were very private—well, maybe not private in the traditional sense but very special to him." She shrugged. "And I don't really know very much about that. I just know he kept some items in a storage locker."

"And would they still be safe there?"

"Sure. Why not?"

He nodded. "So, I hate to say it, but any chance these kidnappers would want the contents of that storage locker?"

She stared at him in astonishment. "I don't think so," she replied slowly. "I can't imagine that there would be …" Her voice had turned cautious, as if she weren't sure.

"And where is this locker?"

"In London," she replied.

"Your father was based out of London?"

"No, it was just one of many places he was based out of at different times," she explained. "He didn't really put down any roots."

"How is that possible? Was he such a vagabond?" He stared at her.

"I know it sounds foolish, but my father was on the move so much that he kept places like that because they were convenient."

"Well, that makes sense," he noted. "Do you know how many he had?"

She shook her head. "Last I heard, at the time of my mother's death, there were three, but he combined them down to one."

"Good Lord," Hatch said. "I can't imagine managing three storage lockers."

"Maybe not," she replied, "but my mother had all kinds of things she didn't want to get rid of. Things she wanted to have available for later in life, when they retired or at least stayed in one place long enough to enjoy them. She was always against putting all her eggs in one basket."

"Well, I applaud that thinking," he agreed, "but she never had a chance to enjoy her things."

At that, Millie shot him a bitter look. "I know. That is something I'll be keeping in mind when I go through the locker."

"And you'll need to," he admitted, "because presumably there will be bills associated with that locker which you'll have to continue to pay."

She winced at that. "The kidnappers' boss did say something about money, and I told him flat-out that my father didn't have any. He didn't. … That's the thing that I don't really understand about all this. My father never had money, like not much of it anyway. He always needed grant money to do this or the other digs. He was always pushing for more grants and nonprofit donations."

"So, as far as you know, there will be no money in the estate?"

"My mother's estate, maybe," she replied, "but he would have spent that toward more digs, if he could have."

"Did he have access?"

She laughed. "I have no idea. I really don't know anything about my mother's estate. Those topics were a part of my father's private affairs, and he tended to those things himself."

At that, Hatch stared at her. "And what if there was money involved in your mother's estate?"

She shrugged. "Well, it would have gone to him. I mean, he was her husband after all, and they had been married for many years." She shook her head.

"So it all would have gone to him. That's an interesting turn of events," he murmured.

"I don't know what's interesting about it," she replied, "and honestly you're freaking me out talking about it that way."

He smiled gently. "It's just more of what we have to consider, when we look at what's going on here."

"Will you consider any of it?" she asked curiously. "Or will your job be done now that you've rescued me? And my father, … I don't know that we'll ever find his body." She stared off in the distance. "A part of me says he himself would be okay with that too."

"Meaning that he would be okay to spend his life out in the desert?"

"In his death, … yes," she stated. "Most definitely. He would be perfectly happy being out there for all of eternity. Not many people would understand that, but I know that he would be okay with it."

"Well, that's interesting," Hatch murmured. "I hadn't really considered that, but I also don't know how much time and effort can go into searching for him."

"None," she replied bluntly. "I don't think these guys intended for his body to ever be found."

"Are you okay with that?"

She stared at him. "I don't even know. … What I want is all a blur at this point. With your help, I'm coping—to some degree at this moment—so thanks for that," she murmured. "All I can tell you is that everything is just so strange, so off the wall. I'm working on adapting, but I'm definitely not there yet."

He stared at her for a long moment. She was a shadow of the strong vibrant woman he'd met before. "That might be," he agreed, "but you need to speed up the process."

She stared at him in shock. "Why?"

"Because you're not out of danger," he replied, "and, until we can get you back on US soil, we don't dare let you out of our sight."

"Who cares now?" she asked, with a bitterness that surprised him.

"I think a lot of people care," he noted, "and I hate to say it, but they may only care because of whatever your father was involved in. As soon as the US government gets wind of the possibility that he was involved in something shady, it'll require a full-blown investigation."

"And that," she added, "will make the Egyptian government very happy."

"They really hate him that much?"

"I don't know if they really hate him, but he had been a thorn in their side for an awfully long while, and, because of all of his fighting with them, he was always a sore spot," she whispered. "It was very hard on all of us when he became so very vocal about it."

At that, Hatch nodded. "Well, hopefully it won't be anything like that this time."

"This time?"

He nodded. "We have orders to speak to the Egyptian government."

"Well, good luck with that," she quipped. "I just hope you leave me out of it."

Hatch nodded. "We'll try. I'll speak to them first, while Corbin stays here with you. Then I'm sure the Egyptian government will also want to speak with Corbin. So I'll return here after my appointment with them, so Corbin can speak with them. Even after all that, they probably want to hear your story out of your own mouth. Sorry."

"When?"

"I'm scheduled soon, starting at eleven a.m., and I expect to be gone for hours. You know how the government types can be."

She nodded. "I don't want to deal with them."

"I understand that. Believe me. I can tell them you are

mourning the loss of your father. That may buy you a couple days. However, I don't expect them to care. So what if we can't talk them out of speaking with you?" he asked.

She gave him a flat stare. "Tell them no. Don't give in to them. As far as I'm concerned, they don't even need to know I'm alive."

CHAPTER 8

MILLIE WOKE UP early that next morning to find herself once again wrapped up in Hatch's arms. She lifted her head and stared at him. "I'm not sure what happened." Yet it felt right, normal. At that glance at his face she remembered him.

"Well, you fell asleep and then started crying," he explained, his voice gentle. "You only calmed down when I picked you up."

"I'm sorry." She looked away from him. "I don't know that something like that has ever happened before. How embarrassing." Yet it wasn't. It was lovely.

"Well, keep in mind you haven't been kidnapped and lost your father before either," he noted. "Don't worry. It's not a problem."

She scrambled off his chest and looked around. They were still in her bedroom, where she vaguely remembered coming back here to rest. She couldn't while Corbin was here, but once Hatch returned … She sat on the edge of the bed and gave herself a mental shake. "You've been beyond kind," she said. "I'm sorry for being such a watering pot."

"Don't apologize for crying. You've been very stressed and overwhelmed. Plus, you are grieving—doubly so, in a way," he noted. "If you're ready to get up again, I'll leave you to it."

She nodded. "I guess I am. I don't even know what I'm supposed to do right now." She stared at him.

He nodded. "Well, clean clothes may go a long way to making you feel better."

"Oh my goodness, that sounds better than it should." She still wore his T-shirt. She flushed with embarrassment. "Wow," she said, more to herself than him, "this is very unlike me."

"Again stress and circumstances." He calmly got up and walked to the other side of the bed and held out some clothes for her. "Corbin bought you one outfit, so you have something clean to wear. You'll feel better once you're dressed."

"I will, indeed. Good thing your shirt is as long as it is."

He smiled. "No worries. Besides, it's never looked even half as good on me."

She laughed. "Well, at least I can get dressed properly now." She watched as he left and then sagged in place. "Dear God, Millie, what the hell's going on with you?" But she knew, and he was right about the grief. Plus the shock and other reactions were all great excuses, but it was definitely time to pull herself up by her bootstraps now and try to get back to normal. Whatever that would be for her now.

Even though America was her home, all she could think about at present was heading back to England to her father's locker, where she might find some answers. At least that's what she considered as she got fully dressed in new clothes—leggings, T-shirt, and underclothes—which she was most grateful to have available again. As she stepped out of the bedroom, she heard Hatch and Corbin discussing arrangements for her to return stateside. She had no time to think it through, but she spoke loudly. "No."

At that, Hatch looked over at her, as she stepped from her bedroom. "Sorry?"

"No," she repeated more firmly.

"No what?" he asked, looking at her and waiting.

"I need to find answers first." Immediately he shook his head, but she glared at him, "Yes," she stated. "I need to know what happened with my father. And to my mother, for that matter."

"Well, that's not something that you'll necessarily find out anyway," he noted cautiously.

"I know," she admitted, "but I also don't want you sending me off while all this is still in a mess. What happens if they kidnap somebody else? Killing the foreman? … That shouldn't have happened."

"No, it shouldn't have," Hatch agreed, "but killing the foreman doesn't mean that it's your job to fix this broken mess."

She glared at him. "Maybe not, but I also need to know what happened and what my father's involvement means in all of this."

"Ah! Now that," Hatch said, "is a whole different story."

She sat down beside him. "You came here to get me."

"We did"—Hatch nodded—"and we've done our job."

"No," she argued. "The job is half done. My father's body is out in the desert somewhere, and I want it back. He may well prefer to stay there, but I need to find out what happened to my father. And, if you won't help me, I'll just have to do it on my own."

Hatch stared at her, shook his head. "You know that's not smart. Plus it is likely your emotions are talking right now. I get it, but you also must be sensible. The Egyptian government will let you leave, but they don't want to see you back here again."

"You mean, I'll be painted with the same brush that they think my father deserved? Even after his death and even though nothing concrete at this point indicated he was involved in anything shady?"

He nodded slowly. "Can you blame them?"

"No, I can't blame them," she agreed quietly, "but neither do I want to believe it."

"What will it take for you to believe your father's involvement in any of this?"

"I don't want to believe any of it," she cried out. "Can't you understand my need to find out the truth?" She looked over at Corbin, or at least she thought that's what his name was. "Surely you can understand that."

"I can understand it." Corbin nodded. "But are you sure you understand what you're asking us to do here? You already know how dangerous this is. You're the one who's only just escaped," he noted. "I doubt your kidnappers will let you escape a second time."

She blanched slightly. "Meaning that, if they find out what I'm doing—" She stopped.

"Think about it. Either they let you go or are definitely aware that you have escaped one way or the other. They are the ones who want to take you out so you don't say anything, or they may well get pissed off that you decided to find answers on your own." Corbin shrugged. "Either way, they're playing for keeps. ... Your father and his foreman are evidence of that. They don't know for sure if you were telling the truth about knowing nothing about this other site, and who knows if they are still seeking proof of that. Maybe they allowed you to escape to follow you to this new dig site."

She thought about it, while Corbin continued to sketch it out for her.

"You escaped. They let you go. Now, if you poke around to find answers, you don't have any leverage. They might have waited a day to kill your father, but circumstances have changed, and they won't think twice before deciding to take you out."

She nodded, struggling to find a way to make them understand, when Hatch gently took her hand. She stared down at his fingers and groaned. "I don't know how to explain it to you, but I feel like a gaping wound's in my heart, after finding out that my mother was murdered, … by this guy, or at least by somebody who worked for him." Shrugging, she continued. "I don't think that makes him any less guilty, but I don't really understand the circumstances." She closed her eyes, took a deep breath. "I need to know more."

"I'll tell you what," Hatch suggested. "How about if we compromise?"

Immediately she looked up at him and stared intently. "What kind of a compromise?"

"We'll push back your flight for forty-eight hours," he offered, "and that's it. We can stall using all kinds of excuses, like maybe you need a little more time to recover or whatever, but we'll never get any more time than that." He continued. "We'll do what we can to help you get those answers, but, when that time is up, there'll be no arguments, no fuss, no fight. You'll get on that plane with us, and we take you back to England."

She stared at him. "England? Not the US?"

"Oh." He turned around to face her fully. "I just assumed you wanted to go to England to retrieve the contents of your father's locker."

She thought about it. "I'll need to do that. Maybe I'll find the answers there."

"So, do you want to go there first maybe?" he asked.

She shook her head. "I won't be allowed back here for a very long time, so I better stay while I can."

"That's quite possibly true," Hatch agreed. "So that's the deal. What do you think?"

She looked over at Corbin, who studied her with interest. "I don't know where my ID and passport are. Maybe still in my suitcase, but without it, we could have a lot of trouble taking me anywhere. Are you okay with that?"

Surprised that she would even ask him, Corbin nodded slowly. "We both understand the need to find answers," he stated. "And, if you follow along with your part of the bargain, we'll do everything we can for you. But, like Hatch said, … you have to agree to get on that plane when it's time. Otherwise you're putting all of us in danger. And we have a few workarounds for your passport, but best if we can find yours."

"Sure. Get my suitcases and with any luck it will be there. Still I don't want to get on that plane without answers," she said. "I could just stay behind, and you guys could leave to find the answers we need," That earned her a dark look from both men. "You don't have to stay. You've done your job. You did rescue me."

"Enough of that talk." Hatch didn't even attempt to keep the harshness out of his tone. "We are not leaving you over here unprotected. That is guaranteed to result in you going missing again, and nobody will find you this time."

She winced at that, thought about what he'd offered, and realized that it really was not only a fair offer but, with their help, she had a much better chance of actually getting some answers. She took a deep breath and then nodded. "Fine, I agree."

"Without argument?" Hatch reaffirmed.

She nodded. "Yes, without argument."

"Good enough." He looked over at Corbin. "You good with that?"

Corbin nodded. "Yeah."

"Done. But now that we're under a forty-eight-hour time frame," Hatch noted, "we better get at it."

HATCH LOOKED OVER at Corbin and saw the acknowledgment in his gaze. He turned back to Millie. "Any chance you would recognize this guy again?"

"What guy?" she asked, looking at him in confusion, as she sipped her coffee.

"The boss."

She blinked and then slowly nodded. "I think I would. He wears a white panama hat, and it was dim in that cave, but I still saw his features."

"Which is interesting in itself. He wouldn't have let you go if he thought you could recognize him."

Corbin spoke up right away. "He didn't think she would survive, didn't suspect that she would recognize him, or didn't figure he would be anywhere around where she would be a danger to identifying him." Corbin's logic was right along the lines of what Hatch was thinking.

At that, she stared at the two of them. "I didn't even think about that, but he had a very American voice—and accent too."

"And what about his looks?"

"He could have been Egyptian. He could have been—" She held up both of her hands. "I don't know. He could have passed for nearly any nationality. Honestly he had darker skin, but so could anybody who had spent a lot of time out in the sun here."

"Do you know if his hands were well-worn, had calluses, or any markings in particular?"

She stared at him. "I couldn't see that closely."

"He's probably thinking that you probably couldn't see very much at all."

"Well, I did see some things," she noted, thinking about it. "He did not have a mustache. He had black hair." She frowned. "But then most everybody here does. He was built but not buff, and he was ..." She thought about that and added, "I don't know what age to be exact, but ... let me think a minute." Closing her eyes for a moment, she took a deep breath. "I would say he was younger than my father, and I'm thinking he was probably in his early or maybe mid-forties. What he did have was an interesting sense of humor and a calmness to him—a definite sense of power around him."

"So, likely the boss was used to being in control, and that happens to be somebody who is used to having everybody else jump when he speaks?" Hatch asked Millie.

"Exactly. The guards followed his orders without any argument, discussion, or even a question. Basically, when he said do something, they got up and did it."

"And would you recognize them? Any of his men?"

She thought about it. "Yes, definitely the one man I saw more often than the others. He wouldn't be that hard to recognize. He is big, and he spoke mostly the local language, although he definitely knew some English, though I don't recall him speaking it. I think he understood it and just didn't talk very much at all."

"But the boss spoke English to him?"

"Yes." She frowned.

"Now what?" he asked because she had a thoughtful look on her face.

"I'm just trying to remember whether he spoke any other language to that one guard, but I don't think so."

"So two guys were looking after you?"

"I only saw the two guards, plus their boss," she stated.

Corbin spoke up. "I can hack into the Egyptian law enforcement database and look for people with any criminal past related to excavation thefts and irregularities."

She nodded. "More than that, see if you can find a database of everybody who's working on these sites. The one guard more than anybody else would have had some dig experience."

"Why do you think that?"

"He was heavily muscled. Like older, grizzled, and his hands were well worn, as if he were using them for more manual labor than any of the other guards. I suspect that he was probably a local and had done his time on the digs himself."

Corbin was already pulling up lists of files on his laptop. "Yet you've been here many months, and you didn't recognize him."

"That's right," she agreed, "so maybe he isn't a local. But the work part and his looks are true enough. Chances are, he was traveling with the boss or could just be staying away from the limelight. Also millions of people live and work here," she noted, "not to mention tourists."

"And, of course, the tourists are a big part of everybody's business."

"Sure, but the locals don't want it to be." She smirked. "It's the tourist dollars everybody works to get, but you can bet an awful lot of locals would just like every tourist to disappear off the face of the Earth."

"But leave their money behind."

"Exactly," she agreed in a dry tone. "Yet you can't blame the Egyptians for it. It's the same in every part of the world."

"No, you're quite right there," Hatch agreed. "It's a tourists' curse—or maybe a blessing. It depends on the point of view of the beholder."

"And here even more so. That was one of the arguments my father had. He always hated some of these sites opening up to the tourists, but, at the same time, he also felt the government wasn't doing justice to their finds because they were spreading things out over time in order to keep the buzz going. With each new discovery, instead of it being publicized or written about, the government was keeping everything in check, until such time as they would let out new information, trying to get the same tourists to return to look at something new and different. My father felt that was all a marketing ploy, and he didn't want to play politics."

"Of course it is a marketing ploy," Corbin admitted, without looking up. "Everybody here has bills to pay, and, like you said, it's the tourists' dollars that pay for it."

"I agree with that," she admitted. "My father and I had more than a few differing opinions when it came to the government, but, from his perspective, it was very much a case of he was right, and everybody else in the world was wrong."

At that, Hatch laughed. "We've seen a few people like

that too."

"It's hard not to in this world. When you think about it, so many people have very set opinions, and they don't really care about anybody else and what they might have to say."

She had said it in such a way that Hatch could tell that the father-daughter relationship she and Marcus had shared probably hadn't been easy. "When you say your father changed, and, having now gone down this pathway, do you think it had something to do with your mother's death?"

She looked startled for a moment, as she stared at Hatch. "I really don't even want to consider what he did *going down this pathway.*"

"I know that," Hatch replied calmly, "but being blind to some telltale signs in front of us, like this guy having kidnapped you in order to get at your father's information, won't help. So you do need to consider everything, even if it means considering something distasteful, then discarding it as unfounded."

"Which I've already done," she announced.

"No," he argued, "you just discarded it. I don't think for a moment that you actually considered it."

She stared at him, and he watched as her shoulders dropped. "Fine," she muttered, "but this isn't easy."

"It's never easy," he replied gently, "but wouldn't you rather know the truth?"

"I thought I wanted to know the truth," she added, "until the truth started to look like this."

At that, he smiled gently. "I would like to track down the men who held you captive," Hatch stated. "They will lead us to the man in the panama hat responsible for you being kidnapped. So you better think about what I just said. It will help you get perspective and will prevent you from being blindsided in the future."

And, with that, they got to work.

CHAPTER 9

MILLIE VIEWED SCREEN after screen, and faces just skipped by. She was having no luck, until suddenly she did. When she stopped, scrolled back, and studied the face closely, she tapped the laptop screen in front of her and called out excitedly, "This is him!"

Immediately both Hatch and Corbin got up from where they were working and sat down beside her. They looked at the man's face, as she nodded. "This is the one who guarded me. This was my jailer."

"So, one down. One to go."

"Nice job," Corbin pitched in.

"Yes, but he is the one I saw more often than not," she explained. "As I think about it, the other guy was more likely the boss's assistant. This one was more of a henchman."

"We have a name." She tapped down below.

"Got it." Hatch noted his features. "We'll run this name through other databases and see what we can come up with."

"*Aman*," he stated, though he couldn't even begin to pronounce the last name.

"It's a fairly common last name though," she noted.

"That's fine," Hatch replied. "We'll do a search and see what we can come up with." With that, Corbin set off to hunt down Aman.

She looked over at Hatch. "I guess this helps, doesn't it?"

she asked.

"It helps a lot," Hatch murmured. "When you think about it, finding out who held you is at the heart of all this."

"I just wish they'd explained what they were after. My father said something about a site he knew something about from the pub, but he didn't tell me anything about it."

"No need for him to do so, as long as he didn't think you had anything to do with it. The less people who knew, the better. In a way he was doing you a favor."

She shuddered. "I get that. I really do. He wasn't a bad guy"—her fingers making quotes in the air—"but, at the same time, it's hard for me to see him as a good guy."

"I didn't say he was a good guy." Hatch smiled. "Far from it. He just didn't want to bloody his hands any more than he had to, and that was a saving grace for you. He could've beaten the crap out of you, the same as they did your father," he reminded her.

She winced. "I know, and it's a hard thing to think about. My father had a lot of failings, but, at his core, something was very good about him."

"You better hold on to that," Hatch noted, "because some pretty unsettling truths could be coming out, in which case, you'll need to focus on remembering your father and all the good things about him."

"Do you think he really was involved?"

"I don't know," he replied. "If he was involved, I guess I'd have to understand why. If he was somebody who cared about all these antiquities and preserving all this history, why he would do something like stealing them is beyond me at this point." Then he stopped, looked at her. "Unless, … unless he really thought the government was so corrupt that somebody like him needed to go private to protect these antiquities on his own."

She stared at Hatch and then frowned. "You know what? That almost sounds like him."

"*Almost* sounding like him is one thing," he stated. "*Sounding* like him can mean all kinds of things."

"He did really hate the Egyptian government," she muttered, hoping Marcus hadn't done anything stupid.

"Of course he hated the government." Hatch chuckled. "Lots of people do. Though most of them don't end up getting into so much trouble."

"No, no, that's quite true," she murmured. "I don't know what to say. I mean, a part of me … sees him for what he was, and another part sees him for the man I knew. And I'm left trying to reconcile it with what everybody else is saying about him."

"But is it everybody or is it just the one?"

"Just the one." Then, with a note of relief, she added, "And that helps. Maybe my father wasn't this horrible corrupt person they were trying to make him out to be. I know what he was like when he had a bottle, and he was more difficult these last few years."

"It's also quite possible that he was hiding antiquities, hoping that maybe he could find a way to bring them out later or to preserve them for later, just to stop the Egyptian government from making a big publicity scene out of these finds."

She stared at Hatch, wondering at his insights. This man who saw too much, understood so much, and seemed to care even more. At least about her. She didn't imagine any other government agents—certainly not those Egyptian government officials she had met recently—would have cared for her like Hatch had or would have been willing to help her by giving her these extra days. She really appreciated it. "That is also something he would do," she admitted quietly. "He often talked about how corrupt the Egyptian government was and how somebody needed to step in and to fix things."

"Your father has an Egyptian background, I understand."

"His grandfather," she murmured. "My great-grandfather. They were quite close for the little time period that he knew him. But apparently it had a huge effect on him because this is where he ended up for his career."

Just then Corbin nodded. "Okay, got Aman. The picture you ID'd is of a guy who has been in trouble with the law and had been fired from a couple digs."

"What for?"

"Stealing antiquities." Corbin raised his head. "It was never proven in court, but he was suspected of finding things and taking them for himself."

"Interesting," she murmured. "That's definitely frowned upon by the Egyptian government. They hold that up as one of the highest crimes."

"Of course they do," Hatch agreed with her. Turning to Corbin, Hatch asked, "Did it give a last known address or anything?"

"I've got a last known address, but wait a sec and let me run it through another database here." He sat for a moment, watching his screen, then shrugged. "This says the property is still occupied, but I can't guarantee that he currently lives there anymore."

"No, he probably doesn't." Hatch frowned. "Family?"

"Yeah, we've got one brother. Maybe we should go have a talk with him."

"That would be doable," Hatch murmured. "Doesn't

mean the brother will be too interested in talking about Aman."

"Maybe not."

"What about me?" she asked. "I'm the injured party here."

"He definitely won't want to talk to you or about you. That's for sure," Hatch stated.

She frowned and nodded. "So, what do we do?"

"Well, we need to track him down, so we can find out what he's up to and where he's staying at the moment. … That's paramount."

Corbin stood. "I'll take care of it." And, with that, he was gone.

She looked over at Hatch in surprise. "What's all that about?"

"He'll go track down the brother and have a talk with him."

"What does have-a-talk-with-him really mean?" she asked cautiously.

Hatch smiled. "We almost never kill people, if we don't have to."

Her eyes widened. "If that's supposed to sound reassuring, it wasn't successful."

He chuckled, leaned over, and gave her a quick hug. "You're fine. And, no, we just want to know if he's willing to talk or not. Sometimes people will talk when things are low-key and quiet, especially when it's just the two of them."

She nodded. "Maybe, but it doesn't sound like this guy would necessarily want to talk at all."

"In that case, he might need a little persuasion. So, in that situation, Corbin will use money first."

"That will work," she admitted, "particularly if there are

any financial issues, which is usually the case here most of the time." Hatch shrugged and didn't say anything to that. "You can go with Corbin, you know? I'll be just fine here alone." She motioned to the rooms around them.

He shook his head. "Nope, that's not happening."

She glared at him. "I don't exactly need a babysitter, you know?" He just gave her that flat stare. She winced. "Okay, so maybe I *did* need a babysitter, but I shouldn't need one now. It's not like I'll go anywhere."

"Actually I should ask you if you wanted to go somewhere. Do you need any supplies for the next day or two?"

She thought about it. "Do you know of any drugstore in the area? It wouldn't be a bad idea, and maybe a little more variety of clothing couldn't hurt. I suppose there's no chance of getting my own clothing back is there?"

He frowned at that. "My team was checking into that. Let me find out." He walked over to the laptop and quickly started tapping on the keys.

She got up and walked behind him. "What are you doing?"

"Just checking with my bosses to see where your personal belongings ended up."

"Do we want to let anybody know that I'm alive and well?"

"Nope, but my bosses are a different story," he explained cheerfully. Within a few seconds he got a response. He nodded, not saying anything, but kept on tapping. Then he looked over at her with a smile. "Your belongings are on the way here."

She stared at him in shock. "Just like that?"

"Well, not quite, nothing is *just like that*, but we'll get them soon enough," he noted. "Now, if you want food or any other supplies, I can't take you anywhere, but, if you need or want something, I would have no trouble getting it delivered to you here."

"You can't take me anywhere? Is that to keep me hidden?"

"Partially," he replied. "Think about it. We've been asking a lot of questions. A whole lot of people are interested in your whereabouts."

"And we don't want to let them know?" she asked cautiously.

"Not yet. I also don't want to leave you alone and have somebody find out about you and maybe decide you had something to do with the foreman's death."

She stared at him, her color fading. "That would not be good."

"No, it sure wouldn't be."

She dropped into the chair beside her. "I was hoping to let my friends know." She stared at him, disconcerted at staying hidden. However, staying for a few days with this man? No problem. ... *Staying hidden?* Well, that put a different spin on it.

"Which friends?" he asked curiously.

"Back in England."

"I would hesitate to let you do that just yet."

She looked over at him. "Is there a particular reason why?"

"Because we don't know the whereabouts of the person who kidnapped you. I would just as soon not let anybody know until we get back to England. He could have connections there, you know."

"Fine," she murmured.

"Do you know where your father's locker is?"

She nodded. "Yes, I've been with him there a couple times. He wouldn't let me inside, but I know the building, the address."

"Does anybody else know about your father's locker?"

She shook her head but then stopped. "I would say no because I don't know of anybody with knowledge of it, but I can't guarantee that. He may have had employees or friends there. I would like to get there sooner rather than later." He frowned at her, but she shook her head. "No, I'm not leaving here until we get answers."

"And what if we can't get answers?"

She repeated, "I've got the forty-eight hours. I'm not talking about more than that. And, speaking of which, couldn't we be doing something, while Corbin is off doing his thing?"

"Well, right now," Hatch said, "we're waiting for your stuff to arrive, and, after that, we'll see. Tell me the names of everybody you worked with when on digs with your father, and think about anybody you might have been suspicious of."

"Suspicious in what way?" she asked curiously.

"Somebody who didn't like your father or who might have been plotting behind his back. We are looking for somebody who might have done something illicit, maybe smuggling drugs with the antiquities, things like that. Somebody who might have had a sketchy past, with a criminal record or something."

She stared at him. "Well, a criminal record is a different story. My father hired a couple people like that."

"Interesting," he murmured. "Why would he do that?"

She shrugged, frowning. "I have no idea. Remember. Hiring wasn't part of my job. In fact, I wonder how I heard of this. Maybe talk among the crew. I don't know. However, you would think, with the local economy being so depressed, that anybody would have jumped at the chance to work for him—even though he was a bear at times."

"Okay, and having hired those people, did you ever have any trouble with them?"

She shrugged. "I didn't deal directly with the workers. Again, our foreman dealt with everyone."

"So, you don't really know if there was any trouble or not?" She shook her head. "What about your father? Did he use a laptop? Did he have anything to do with computers and such?"

She stared at him, clapping her hand over her mouth. "What happened to my father's gear?" she cried out, bolting to her feet.

"There was no record of any electronics left behind in the hotel. That's another reason why everybody thought that you guys had run off."

She shook her head. "We didn't run anywhere," she snapped. "We were taken."

"And I get that," he murmured. "That's not what I'm saying."

She sighed. "I'm sorry. It's still such a stressful thing. I shouldn't be jumping on you. You've been lovely to me. But my father did have a laptop," she murmured. "And a cell phone, which we both used." She glared around. "I gather that's not coming with my clothing."

"Unlikely," he said quietly. "We won't know until it gets here of course. However, I would think that, no matter who kidnapped you, the electronics would have been one of the first things they would have wanted access to."

"Right," she agreed.

"Do you know any of the log-ins?"

"Yes, of course." She looked up at him in surprise. "One of the things that I always insisted on was memorizing my passwords because you never really know who to trust in this world. I had a bad scenario when I was in university, where I had my laptop stolen, and people got into my bank accounts, and it was just a mess," she explained. "I learned my lesson early on."

"Well, not everybody has learned it. Even now," he said, with a smile.

"Once you get in trouble, it's pretty easy to make it a priority."

"I wish more people would do that as a preventative measure," he noted. "Too often it's not an issue until it becomes a huge pain in the ass."

"That's always the way," she muttered.

He continued. "If you had a laptop, where could you find more information about the people who either worked with you or your father?"

"Well, I have his email access," she shared, as he stared at her. She shrugged. "He didn't take much time to do basic correspondence, so I did it for him."

He motioned at her. "You want to open that up then?"

She nodded and, using his laptop, quickly logged into her father's email. She winced. "Like sixty emails are here," she cried out.

"Well, considering his life, that's not necessarily unexpected, is it?"

"No," she agreed. "I would normally keep track of a lot of this for him."

"So you did have a lot to do with him in that way then."

"Well, in some ways," she agreed, "but, I mean, when

you think about it, it didn't seem like it was that big of a deal."

"No, but it let you have access that I'm not sure your kidnappers had any idea of."

She stared at him. "They didn't even ask me."

"That's because, in the boss's mind, he couldn't imagine ever allowing his daughter or anyone else to have access to his emails."

"Doesn't that also lend weight to the idea that my father was innocent?"

"I don't think *lending weight* to any of this is really part of the issue right now," he stated. "We're still way too far out in the weeds right now with our lack of information, and we have no plausible ideas yet. More so, we have no working theory to see what might have gone down." He motioned at the laptop. "So go through the emails and see if there's any inclination of or any warning of a looming threat."

As she went through them, she frowned. "You know what? In all the time that I worked for him, I never saw anything like that."

"That's fine. Do you know if he had another email address?"

She shook her head. "I don't think so."

"But you don't know for sure, do you?"

"No, I don't." She went through the emails while he sat and read a little bit over her shoulder, but most of it was pertinent to the dig itself and to grants. "Like I said, he was always fussing over grants."

"And presumably he needed to."

"Yes, at least I thought so," she noted. "In our world, grant money is the end-all of everything." He nodded without saying anything. She looked over at him. "What are you thinking about?"

"May I have the laptop for a moment?" he asked.

She nodded and handed it over. He immediately went into the settings to check if any other emails were downloaded or forwarded to the same email. And, sure enough, found another one. But it was inactive. He logged out of the email she'd been into, then brought up the new email address. "Do you want to try logging into this one?"

She quickly logged into it, using the same password, then frowned as several more emails downloaded. "How is it that I didn't know about this one?"

"Well, he either knew when to expect messages or knew when to not have these download around you," he suggested. "Maybe he had a notification on his phone, and then he quickly deleted them or dealt with them himself. Or maybe he forwarded them and then dealt with them later on." He frowned. "There are all kinds of ways around this stuff, which you know better than I do. You also weren't looking for deceit, so you might not have been fussing with it."

"No, I sure wasn't," she mumbled.

He tapped the screen. "And this unfortunately is not what you want to see."

She stared at him and then snatched the laptop back. As she read through these messages, he walked around the room and watched her closely.

HATCH WATCHED THE color slide from her cheeks.

"Wow," she whispered in shock. "He's talking about moving antiquities out of the country."

"Exactly, and somebody involved in that operation

probably told."

"Of course." Millie stared at Hatch in shock. "If I'd known, I'd have told as well. That is one of the biggest taboos. We always have problems with theft, with people picking up hidden little trinkets, when they should be passing them over. You do the best you can, but there'll always be that certain element of criminal life that doesn't want to play fair. And, of course, to them, playing fair doesn't equate because they're not getting paid enough compared to what they see as riches being moved in and out."

"So, if somebody thought he was being shafted by your father, he could easily have turned on him. Keep looking through those emails," he murmured. "And, if you don't want to do it, I will."

"No," she snapped, her voice hardening. "I need to figure this out."

He didn't say anything more but sat beside her and watched as she brought up emails. He read what he could, bits and pieces, but knew that more and more of it was just breaking her heart. "Try to figure out what Marcus's mindset was at the end." And her mental state was worrying now, as Hatch stepped up behind her and gently massaged her knotted neck and shoulders.

She leaned back and closed her eyes and whispered, "I don't care what his mind-set was. It was wrong, pure and simple."

"What I meant is to make sure if there is any chance that whatever he did," he murmured, "was something he was forced into or otherwise coerced into doing."

"I don't know. I see no sign of that in these emails," she murmured. "But it's obvious that he was participating in moving some of these antiquities out of the country."

"What was he doing with them? That is the million-dollar question now." She read off an address from one of the secret emails. He nodded. "I'll look that up. It's a commercial warehouse district out of England."

She stared at him. "And a little too close to his locker, I suppose."

"You tell me." Hatch faced at her. "Do you know the address?"

She opened up the other email account. "I have it written down in one of my emails," she murmured.

"Any reason why?"

"Yeah, I often email information to myself, so I don't lose it."

He nodded. "That just means that, if somebody else gets your laptop, they can get access to it."

"But it wasn't mine in the first place," she stated. "I just didn't want to lose track of where stuff was, in case something did happen to my father. Once you suddenly lose one parent, and you only have one left, you tend to take a few more precautions."

He sat back down beside her and waited. She brought up the email with the locker address and read it off to him. He quickly typed it into Google Maps and whistled. "They're on the same block."

She stared at him and shook her head. "No, no, no, please not."

"Go through the emails again," he said, "looking for anything there that gives an indication of why."

"Nothing like that is in these emails." She scrubbed at her face with both hands. "All I can think of was the last series of fights with the Egyptian government, where he was accusing them of stealing antiquities that needed to be preserved. So turning around and doing that himself is just—"

"Would he have taken them out of the country in order to preserve them?"

She looked at him sadly. "You know what? He probably would have. I just didn't ever have any inkling that he would have gone this far."

"But somebody knew. And now whoever it is who kidnapped you, were they looking for a new dig site, or were they just trying to find his stash?"

"I don't know." She looked back at him in confusion.

"Think about what you were asked while you were there with the kidnappers. Was there any inclination or any talk of storage space or a locker or you know, … a warehouse or anything similar?"

She stared at him. "I don't think so, but he didn't talk to me much about it."

"He was probably just trying to gauge whether you were involved or not. And I would hazard a guess that your father made it very clear that you didn't know anything."

She stared at him, and her bottom lip trembled almost immediately. She exerted enough control to stop it. "I don't want to cry anymore. I need to understand what's happened."

"In case you haven't noticed, we're getting there," he noted. "Do you have any other information on your father that would not necessarily be accessible by, … say, law enforcement?"

She looked at him in confusion.

"You know, like online files, cloud storage, or anything that might give us more information about what he was doing and where. Those emails didn't have any details."

She shook her head. "No, they were simple shipping and receiving, and that's it."

"And, of course, they'll hide a lot of what he was doing."

"Not only that," she added, "some of this stuff was coming back and forth through the import-export company."

"Which one?" he asked. When she gave him the name, he immediately typed it in and nodded. "Imperial Exports."

"What does that even mean?" she asked.

"It means, it's a cover for all kinds of stuff. We'll hunt down more information on this." He sent the information to Killian.

"Can you just get information like that?"

"If the information is available?" He nodded. "Yes. Lots of times it isn't though."

When answers came back almost five minutes later, he whistled. "Looks like, this time, we are in luck. Apparently absolutely no penalties have been levied against Imperial Exports. Nobody has any problems with them, and they pay their taxes. Interestingly they've been around for ten years." He looked over at her. "That is another suspicious duration, don't you think?"

Her face paled, and she nodded. "It is." She swallowed. "What on earth was my father thinking of?"

"Or was he even thinking at all?"

"I don't know," she replied. "Like I said, his behavior got a lot worse over these last years since Mom's death."

"And now that you know that she was murdered, is there any chance he thought it might have been connected to these antiquities?"

"It's quite possible."

"How so?"

"I don't know if he knew that this was the guy who killed her—or had her killed at least." She waved her hand. "I don't even know what to think about that." In the middle of her speech, she yawned. She stared out at nothing, looking irritated. "Why am I still so tired? And don't go saying shock or reaction." At that, he shrugged and didn't say anything. She glared at him. "Is that what you think it is?"

"Well, it makes sense to me," he replied gently. "When you've been through such an ordeal, it's not like you'll recover instantly."

"No, but I need to recover faster than this."

"You're not going anywhere for a couple days," he noted. "Remember that."

Her shoulders slumped again. "I know, but I can't just sit here. while you do everything for me."

"Why not?" he asked. "Hey, I haven't looked after anybody in quite a while. It's all good."

"Who have you ever looked after?" she asked.

"I watched my kid sister when she got sick one summer. Our parents went to Europe, so it was just the two of us. She was seventeen and professed to be an adult who didn't need my attention, but when she got sick? She became this little girl again. It helped us reconnect in ways that I hadn't even thought about until then. When she got sick, we both realized how far apart we had grown." He smiled. "While she recuperated, we had a wonderful time."

"Sounds like you had a great relationship with her."

"We did." He gave her a half shrug. "Still do actually."

"I missed that," she murmured.

He frowned. "Missed what?"

"I missed having a sibling." She shrugged. "It was just me and my parents, and you know they weren't the easiest."

"You mentioned you spent a lot of time in boarding schools."

"Yes. Most of my life, if the truth be told," she admitted, "and that's wasn't easy either."

"I'm sorry," he said. "It sounds like you didn't have the easiest childhood."

"There were some great things about it." She gave him a big smile. Then she thought about it for a moment and sighed. "Then there were a lot of things that really sucked."

"Like when your parents were out on digs?"

"If they were on a dig, and I could join them, that was fine," she shared, "but there were lots of times they were too busy."

The way she said *busy* told him so much. "As it turns out, my parents traveled a lot too," he noted.

"How come?"

"Mostly for business. My dad was a geologist, and he had his own exploration company. My mom always traveled with him, and that left us kids sometimes with aunts and uncles, but the two of us were very close, and that made up for a lot of it."

She nodded. "I don't think people should have kids, unless they're prepared to look after them," she announced bitterly.

Hatch agreed, reaching out to hold her hand. He smiled. "Lots of people have kids because it's the thing to do, but then, when they get them, they find they hadn't realized what it entailed and how much it would curb their lifestyles. So they make the best of it by trying to make a compromise between their lives and the lives of their kids."

"Yeah, but all that really means," she said sadly, "is no life for the kids, or at least not one where they spend enough time with their parents …" She yawned yet again.

"I think we've had enough of this. Why don't you close your eyes for a bit and get some rest." She looked up at him, and he saw the weight of the world pulling her down again. "Come on. Just rest." He helped her to her feet, walking her back to the bed, where he sat down beside her. "You're safe now."

"I know," she whispered, "but, every time I close my eyes, something jerks me awake. I am back in that cold dark cave, and I am all on my own. I feel like I'm being buried alive in there."

"And …" he added, "while you rest easy, we've hired a couple locals to see if we could locate where you were held, but they've not found anything yet."

She nodded. "I have no idea how far I walked, but it seemed like he wasn't that far wrong when he said my body would be found down the road at an archeology dig down the road in three thousand years."

"He was wrong." Hatch gently stretched out and joined her on the bed, tugging her beside him.

She shuffled a little bit, so that her head rested against his shoulder. "Hope you don't mind."

"Sleep," he said. "That's what you need most."

"Yeah, and what will I do to sleep when you're not around?"

"What do you mean?"

"Have you not realized that, since you found me, every time I sleep, it seems to be in your arms."

He chuckled. "You know what? I can't see how I'm supposed to get upset about that. You're a beautiful woman. Where's the problem?"

Her lips quirked as he watched. "Maybe there is none.

But, if you have a girlfriend, it may not go over that well."

"No girlfriend," he replied cheerfully. "Single and happily available."

Her lips twitched again. "Is that a hint?"

"I don't know," he replied. "Are you in the market?"

"I don't feel like I'm in the market for much of anything. I feel a bit like damaged goods right now,"

"What happened with your last partner?" Of course he knew from hearing Strand's side but wanted to hear her side of the story.

"We broke up because I was planning to go on a dig, and he wanted me to stay home."

"Well, that was very inconsiderate of him," Hatch noted gently.

Her eyes drooped yet again. "I thought so too, but, hey, he didn't agree."

"Did you break it off?"

"Yeah, I sure did," she stated. "I really wanted somebody who would be a little more accommodating."

"Yet I'm sure he wanted to be around you more than you expected."

"Maybe, I don't know. I just wasn't feeling it. He wanted to get married, and I was not up for that. In the end, that was probably the biggest issue overall."

"Sounds like it was the right thing to do. Why date someone you have no intention of marrying?" He reached up and stroked her hair, helping her to relax further.

"I guess ..." She yawned yet again and snuggled in close to him and fell asleep.

CHAPTER 10

MILLIE WOKE UP from her impromptu nap, started, and realized once again she was completely on Hatch's lap. She stared up at him. "Wow." She immediately tried to pull back.

"Easy, … take it easy," Hatch said. "Wake up first."

She sagged against him, looped an arm around his chest, and yawned. "That's becoming a habit."

"And I'm okay with it." He chuckled.

She smiled and rubbed her cheek gently against his shirt. "Thanks for that. It's embarrassing, you know? I keep crawling onto your lap, every time I fall asleep. Almost like a homing pigeon."

He wrapped his arms around her and tugged her up close. "Obviously some traumas still need to be dealt with, and that will take time."

"You think?" She straightened using his hard chest to push herself upright. "I'm hungry again," she stated abruptly.

"Good," he replied. "I ordered lunch not very long ago. It should be here any second."

Then she noticed her belongings piled at the bedroom door. "Did that come in while I was napping too?"

He nodded. "I had to disturb you, when I got up to bring them in, but, when I returned, that's when you pretty well moved onto my lap."

She shook her head. "Sorry about that."

"It's not a problem," he repeated gently.

She rolled her eyes and then her shoulders.

"Except, it hardly seems to be the best sleeping position for you."

"Maybe not." She smiled. "But it was definitely safe and cozy, so I thank you for that." She got up and stretched. "Any chance I can sort through my stuff?"

"Sure you can," he agreed. "Let's take a look and see if it's all there or if anything important is missing."

"I'll just be happy to have some clothes and some of my personal stuff back, but it's my passport is what worries me," she noted. "It's such an odd feeling to lose it all. Even though each item is inexpensive and easily replaceable, yet, in some way, they feel priceless because, like those days I was a captive, they were stolen from me."

"Understood." And, with that, he picked up the bags, carried them into the other bedroom, and put them on the undisturbed bed. While she inspected her stuff, he just stood to the side and watched.

"Well, I think everything is here," she muttered, looking at her retrieved belongings. "I was in the process of cleaning out some of this stuff anyway," she murmured. "Oh, thank heavens for that. My passport is here." She held it up with a happy grin. "I wasn't sure how you were planning to get me out of here without one. I usually keep it hidden in my suitcase when traveling as purses are easily stolen. However, obviously I don't have my laptop or my dad's phone or my purse."

"No, but I'm pretty sure the kidnappers would have taken any electronics. However, we did claim Marcus's belongings as well, so we have his journals."

A hand rose instinctively to her heart as she nodded, tears in her eyes. "Thank you." She continued to nod. "Thank you. … I'll want to keep those."

Hatch approached her and gave her a hug, waiting for her to process this.

She pulled away from him and nodded. "So, when is the food coming?" Right about then came a knock on the door. She startled at the noise.

"I want you to stay here in the bedroom."

At that, she felt fear sliding into her heart with icy precision. "That's guaranteed to make me not want to answer a door ever again."

"Are you the one who opened the door to your kidnappers?"

She nodded. "Yeah, I didn't have any reason not to."

"Well, you do now," he stated. "Don't ever open a door while you're here." He started toward the front door, listening first, then opening it to find packages of food outside, just waiting for them to be retrieved.

"I like this system," she stated, smelling the air.

He grinned. "Anything within reason we can get," he explained. "We enjoy it while we have it, but it's definitely not the reason we do any of this."

"No"—she nodded—"though I can't imagine why you put yourselves in these dangerous situations."

He looked over at her. "Because it's just what we do. Corbin and I have worked together on missions for the last twelve years," he explained quietly. "At some point in time most people need a change, and this was the change that we got, moving into this special section of the government."

"Is it a change?"

"Not much of one," he admitted on a chuckle. "We're

still out trying to rescue the world but now with less bureaucracy."

"Well, you obviously have a talent for it."

"Hey, you rescued yourself," he reminded her.

She nodded. "Good point." She followed him to the couch and used the coffee table to spread out the food. "What about Corbin?" she asked. "Do we need to save any for him?"

Hatch shook his head. "No, definitely not. He'll grab something while he's out, or we'll get more in when he returns."

"Good." She picked up one of the dishes and started eating. "I wasn't planning on sharing anyway." She flashed Hatch a bright grin.

"I'm glad to see you're feeling better."

She nodded. "That nap seems to have done a lot for me."

"Good," he said. "Has anything else come to mind?"

She shook her head. "No, not yet. I keep hoping but nothing so far."

"Well, it all falls to that locker, it seems."

"I know," she murmured. "I was trying to avoid thinking about that."

"When you have a problem like this, it's best to face it head-on. We need to see what's in that locker, and we need to track down that email we found earlier."

"How do you do that?"

"I already handed it off to the team, and they're tracking it down now." She nodded. "Did your father work with anybody over in England?"

"Not that I know of, but again what do I know?" she murmured sadly. "It seems like my father had a life that didn't have much of anything to do with mine."

"And yet you already knew that in many ways, didn't you?"

"Yes," she agreed, "definitely. I went off and did my own thing, and I guess that opened things up for him to do his own thing." She stopped and stared. "God, that just sounds terrible, doesn't it?"

"In what way?" he asked, as he took a bite of the food in front of them.

"Just ..." She stopped, took a deep breath. "I mean, ... if I had been there more, maybe he wouldn't have gone down this pathway."

"Maybe not, or maybe he had a disease that was already killing him and was making him a little bit crazy," he suggested, with a shrug. "Without his body we can't ever have a postmortem, and, at the rate we're going, by the time we do find it, ... chances are, we won't get much information off it anyway. We do know he had a rickety heart."

"To put it down to an organic problem," she noted, "is a cop-out. And he said nothing about his heart."

He grinned. "It gives you an out in terms of an option," he offered gently. "I wasn't trying to excuse his behavior, but maybe offering ways to try to understand it. Sometimes having a condition, in this case his heart, might explain some of his behavior."

"And trying to understand it would help a lot," she admitted, "because that's the part that I'm really stuck on. Why would a man, who has spent all this time preserving all these artifacts, intentionally do something to damage them?"

"But you don't know that he's damaging them." Hatch's fork froze midair. "Or do you?"

She stared at him. "I don't. But, if the artifacts left the

country, he's taking them away from their rightful owners. So that's just plain and simple theft. In this case, in this country, it's considered quite a nasty crime, with very high penalties."

"And yet he hated the Egyptian government and was quite vocal about them causing all kinds of damage to the industry. So again, I think we're back to the idea that he may well have thought he was helping to protect these antiquities."

"That would be an easier scenario for me to understand," she murmured, "but it's still not necessarily the right one."

"You can't be bothered about right or wrong," he stated. "That isn't the point right now. Just be open and understand what *might* have been going on in his head."

"That's hard to do," she replied, "almost impossible actually, because, well, like I said, … he was a difficult person."

"How much of that difficulty could have been because he was doing something that he knew he shouldn't get involved in and was afraid of getting caught?"

She frowned, as she studied Hatch. "I don't know," she whispered. "I guess that's possible too."

"I'd say it's quite possible, and maybe the best answer you'll get at this point."

"Which isn't much of an answer at all," she noted miserably.

"Maybe not." He grinned. "But, when you think about it, you already got to see your father's body. You know for a fact that he's dead, so you're not looking for closure in that sense. Instead you are looking for closure about why he might have gotten involved in something as distasteful as moving some of these archaeological finds out of the country, calling it *theft*. And yet, if you look at it from another point of view, does him trying to preserve these antiquities make sense to you or not?"

"It does make sense." She sighed. "Maybe he had instructions to bring it all back, if the Egyptian government, you know, cooperated or something." She shook her head. "I have to admit that all of it just, … it just sounds bizarre."

"You don't know of anybody who he worked with here?"

"Not here. He did have a couple friends in England though. He stayed with one of them whenever he was over there."

"Okay, so he didn't work with people in England, outside of this import-export company, but he did have friends."

She nodded slightly. "I guess that's what you meant in the first place, isn't it?"

"No, I meant business associates, but friends are just as good," he stated. When they were almost done eating, his phone buzzed. He pulled it out, took a look, and smiled. "Corbin is on his way back."

She looked down at the food and winced. "We just ate his lunch."

"No, we didn't." When a series of odd taps came at the door, Hatch got up casually and opened the door, letting Corbin in.

Corbin walked in, carrying a bag of food. He looked at them, surrounded by food, and smiled. "Looks like both of us had the same idea."

She gave him a fat grin. "I would be very happy to eat yours as well."

He burst out laughing and then stopped, looked at her cautiously. "I spoke to the brother of your jailer Aman."

She nodded slowly, put down her plate, and leaned toward him. "And?" she asked. "What did you find out?"

Corbin sat down. "So, per his brother, Aman apparently took a job that got him into trouble with the law a long time ago. When I told his brother there were suspicions that Aman may have been involved in the disappearance of you and your father, he just nodded and said he wouldn't be surprised. When I asked him if he would be surprised about Aman being involved in murder, his eyes widened, and he winced, but he just shrugged."

"Did he have any idea where Aman has been staying?"

Corbin nodded, then held up piece of paper. "I've got an address. I took a look and watched it for a bit. It looks like maybe it is some secret hostel, with several people staying there at the moment," he noted. "I'll go back after we eat, hoping a bunch of the people would have moved on by then."

"I'll take a look, while you eat," Hatch offered immediately. "I'd like to get an idea of the layout."

Corbin nodded. "Perfect, your turn." He handed over the address. "I'll eat some food and tank up a bit. Maybe I'll crash for about thirty minutes, and, hopefully by then, you will have contacted me."

At that, Millie looked over at Hatch. "Do you think that's wise? If the brother is in contact with Aman, you could be walking into a trap. What if you waited until nobody is there?"

Corbin laughed. "If it's truly a hostel, people will always be there. Plus, from my surveillance, it's a huge building with a potentially large capacity."

"Don't worry," Hatch told Millie. "In such a huge place, tourists must come and go all the time. I'll be safe, maybe pose as a dig worker."

She snorted at that. "Like hell. Everybody will have you pegged. You look like a foreigner. It doesn't matter if you change your appearance or not. Plus, how much do you even know about the digs?" she asked. "You need to come up with a better, more believable excuse."

"Got it," Hatch replied, smiling at her.

His smiles didn't help. She didn't like this idea at all, and she openly glared at him. "Corbin is on babysitting duty now then, is that it?" She couldn't explain her reticence. "You know it's a bad idea."

"Why is that?" Hatch asked.

"Because Corbin has already been made, and the brother probably tipped off Aman. Now they'll both just be waiting to see who shows up next."

"Well, I'll be next," Hatch said, "and I'll take a look around and get inside and check it out some more."

She glared at him. "You know it's not a good idea."

"It's what we do," he stated. "Have a little faith."

She subsided somewhat. "Fine, but, for the record, I don't like it."

He grinned. "Try to relax. Even nap while I'm gone. You'll feel better."

She slid her gaze over toward Corbin, who was watching their byplay with interest. "That won't happen," she announced, as she crossed her arms over her chest. Hatch was already at the front door, as she added, "I don't feel good about this at all."

He stopped, looked at her, and asked, "In what way?"

"I don't know," she replied. "I just feel like there'll be a reception waiting for you."

He studied her for a long moment. "Okay, thanks for

the warning. I'll see you soon."

Her eyebrows shot up. "Won't you listen to me?"

"I'll take it into consideration," he explained, "because we believe in instincts, but I can't let something like fear stop me."

She felt the heat on her cheeks at that. "That's fair. Obviously I *am* afraid. I've just lost my father, been kidnapped, struggled to find my way back out of the death-trap sand dunes, where I was left to die. Now I just don't want anything to happen to you guys," she muttered.

"I get it. Fear is definitely an issue, but so is self-preservation. It's what I am really good at, and actually … it's what we're both good at. Thank you for caring. I appreciate it." And, with that, he turned and stepped out the door.

She glared at the closed door for a long time, then turned to look at Corbin, who was studying her carefully. "Will he really be careful?"

"Actually, he will," he stated immediately. "Hatch is very good at what he does."

Her shoulders slumped, she muttered, "But everybody gets caught."

"*Sometimes* people get caught," he agreed. "But remember. You also wanted answers."

She flushed at that and stared at Corbin, realizing that, but for her need for answers, they'd be safely away from here. A hard thing to accept. "God, if something happens to him, … I'll be responsible for it, won't I?"

"No." Corbin shook his head. "This is what we do, what Hatch does, so let him go do it."

"What if he gets hurt while he's out there?"

"Then he gets hurt, and we'll do our best to patch him

up."

She stared at him. "What if it's not that simple?"

"So"—he smiled at her—"I gather you like him."

She flushed and then shrugged. "Yeah, well sure. He's a nice enough guy."

"He's more than a nice guy." Corbin chuckled. "He's a really nice guy. And he's all heart."

She glared at him. "I didn't say that I was attracted to him or anything."

"Sweetheart"—he shook his head, with a gentle smile—"you really don't have to try to hide it."

And, with that, he returned to eating the food in his container. She stared at it, but all she could think about was Hatch and whether he would come back, safe and sound.

HATCH QUICKLY RETRACED Corbin's steps and then did a wide circle, approaching the property in question from a different angle. This area was crowded with buildings, cutting down on the sunshine reaching the pathways here. Plus, looking up at the sky, Hatch noted it was overcast. Maybe a rainstorm was moving in. Regardless, it all helped to reduce the impact of the heat for the moment.

He leaned up against the wall and watched his surroundings. Unlike when Corbin had been there, it was pretty quiet right now. Hatch studied the shadows and smiled when one of them moved. The man stepped forward, searching the area around him, before walking up to the property and slipping inside the big wrought iron gate and headed to one of the nearby doors.

From the little bit that Hatch saw of the robed man, it

was Aman, the jailer Hatch was looking for. And that surprised him. He figured Aman would have been long gone by now. That he was still here meant that his boss was likely here too. Or maybe Aman had been left behind to keep an eye on things. Like Millie.

Hatch waited and watched but saw nobody else appear. He stepped forward and quickly entered the same gate. Almost immediately, he came to the door which Aman had chosen earlier. Hatch must get inside unnoticed. He tested the doorknob to find it unlocked and quickly slipped inside.

Somebody shifted, somebody who had been waiting for him and now tried to come after Hatch. He took him down without too much trouble, but, even down there on the ground, Aman looked really big. Hatch stared at him, looking at the fury in his eyes.

The big man glared at him. "Who the hell are you?" he snapped. His accent was guttural and harsh, as though he was capable of speaking English, but it wasn't his language of choice.

"Somebody who's very interested in where you left your kidnap victims, Aman."

He shrugged. "I don't know what you're talking about."

"Good," he replied, "because I want to know everything there is to know, and, if you don't want to tell me, I'm totally okay with that. Although I should warn you that I'm a little pissed about the whole thing."

Aman snorted. "You won't get anything from me."

"Probably not. But once your boss finds out that we've had this little talk, how much will he trust you?"

At that, Aman's gaze widened, but he remained quiet.

"That's what I thought. He's not the trusting type, and he'll want to make sure that you got out of this with the upper hand. Yet I can tell you right now, that ain't happening, buddy."

"You and who else will stop me?" Aman asked. "Do you think I didn't let you take me?"

"Glad to hear that too," Hatch noted. "I'm really quite ready for a bit of a dustup. Assholes like you piss me off, and I could really use a better fight than this one was."

Aman sneered. "You're no different than me."

"You don't know anything about me," Hatch replied.

Aman shrugged. "I don't care to either. You're in my home. You're an intruder and a foreigner," he snapped. "Believe me. All of law enforcement will be on my side."

The thing was, Aman was quite correct on that point. "Oh, I know," Hatch agreed cheerfully. "No disagreement there. I'll just have to make sure you don't get a chance to talk then."

Aman stared at Hatch silently. "I don't know anything about what you're talking about anyway," Aman said.

For the first time, Hatch saw fear in Aman's eyes, and Hatch liked that. "Yeah, of course not. So you know nothing about Marcus and Millie. They were kidnapped, and apparently Marcus is dead now. Where did you dump the body, big guy?"

At that, Aman's eyes widened even farther.

"And, of course, your boss has skipped to England," Hatch added. "We've already tracked his flights, leaving you to face murder charges."

Aman didn't say anything to that either.

"How long before the boss finds out that you're such a loser that you got taken down?"

Still Aman remained silent.

Hatch smiled. "But none of that matters. What I want

to know is where you put Marcus's body and what your boss is doing in England."

"Well, you'll have to kill me for that."

"Except you won't tell me much when you're dead, will you?"

"I won't tell you anyway," Aman snapped. "Do you really think that a man who would kidnap two people will give a shit about what happens to me?"

"Well, he appreciates loyalty over and above everything else," Hatch noted softly. "So just how loyal are you?"

"Very," Aman replied. "I've worked for him for a really long time."

"I know." Hatch nodded. "Got into a lot of trouble, and now even your family doesn't want anything to do with you."

"I don't want anything to do with them either," he snapped.

"Except for your brother, I guess."

Aman hesitated for just a second at that mention of his brother. "They're losers, the whole lot of them."

"Why, because they work for a living?"

"I work too," Aman stated. "I do a hell of a lot better than they do."

"Yeah, but you kidnap innocent women to die in the desert and the old men? You beat them until they die. How noble is that?"

"You don't know anything about it. Marcus was a danger to Egypt."

"Well, if you were working for the Egyptian government, I might give a shit," Hatch admitted, "but, since you work for a guy who only wants what Marcus may have squirreled away, that doesn't endear me to you at all."

"I don't give a damn. You think you know so much, but you don't know shit."

"No, maybe not," Hatch agreed. "But I do know that losers, like you, just don't change their colors. I believe you're the same guy who you were before, Aman, and that's just a liar and a cheating loser."

At that, the other man glared at him.

"So, where is your boss going?"

"I thought you knew he would go to England." He sneered.

Hatch shrugged. "We've got feelers out, but you could save me a lot of time." Aman just stared at him. "Right, so you won't be helpful. You don't care about who you kill in the process, and the fact that you left that poor woman to die in that cave doesn't matter to you in the least."

Aman shrugged. "I didn't kill her."

"No, but you were supposed to, weren't you?" The guy continued to stare at him, mute. "But you couldn't even bring yourself to follow those instructions."

"What? So now I'm too empathetic?" he asked. "You just accused me of being a killer because I left her alone in the cave to die."

"Well, at least you've admitted to doing that much."

Aman immediately clamped his lips together, realizing just how much he had said.

"I already know that it was you, so I wouldn't worry about it. What I do want to know is what else you can tell me."

"I can't tell you anything. I won't tell you anything."

At that, Hatch nodded. "Well, you could, but you don't want to."

"Not much difference," Aman replied. "I talk to you,

and I'm dead."

"Once he finds out you've talked to me at all, death happens anyway," Hatch noted. "From where I sit, you're dead already."

Aman glared at him. "Not if I take you out first."

"Well, that ain't happening." Hatch gave him an eyeroll.

"Says you. Do you think I haven't been up against worse assholes than you?"

"I'm sure you have," Hatch murmured. His muscles were tensed, waiting for Aman to make his move. It would be nice if Hatch had backup, but that wouldn't happen here. And, as relaxed as Aman was underneath Hatch, obviously Aman had something else planned. Hatch quickly glanced around for any other dangers he hadn't seen, but it looked to be a fairly empty building. "You obviously have a lot of confidence in your ability to handle whatever comes your way," Hatch murmured.

"Of course." Aman laughed. "Assholes are everywhere, and, in my line of work, keeping them at bay has always kept me in good stead."

"Sure," Hatch agreed. "As long as you can. It's when you fail that you get into trouble."

Aman shrugged. "Hasn't happened yet."

"Oh, I'm sure somebody in your little corner of the world will tattle about my visit here." Hatch smiled.

Aman shook his head. "No, that won't make any bit of difference. I've worked for him for a long time."

"I know." Hatch nodded. "But, if you won't help me and take this opportunity—" In a sudden move, Hatch quickly hit him hard with an upper cut.

But Aman just stared at him and barely blinked in reaction to being hit.

Hatch sighed. "*Great,* so you think you're a tough guy too, don't you?"

He sneered. "I can certainly handle any of that bullshit you think you're passing my way."

"If you say so." Hatch then hit him again and then again. At the same time, Aman just laid there and didn't even fight back. Hatch knew that he would have to come up with something that shook Aman off balance.

Hatch was used to taking down these big guys. The fact that Aman wasn't even fighting back worried Hatch. Maybe the big guy was waiting for Hatch to wear down. He didn't know. This guy was big and ugly to boot. And, for the first time, Hatch wondered just what he was missing here. When he heard a sound behind him, he ducked and rolled to the right.

And, when the blow came down, instead of hitting Hatch, it hit Aman in the chest.

Hatch bounded to his feet, and, kicking out with a lethal right kick, he cracked the new assailant in the jaw, snapping his head backward, collapsing him to the ground. Then Hatch dropped to Aman, staring up at him, with a knife in his chest.

"Shit." Hatch bounced to his feet. He looked at the second man, unknown to Hatch, and confirmed by the odd angle that his neck was broken. With a groan at the way things turned out, Hatch quickly slipped out the rear of the property and disappeared.

CHAPTER 11

"HATCH SHOULD BE back by now," Millie fretted for the umpteenth time.

Corbin looked over at her and smiled; yet he hadn't said anything the last few times she'd muttered about the delay. When the door opened suddenly, and Hatch slipped inside, she raced over and threw her arms around him.

"Are you okay?"

He wrapped his arms around her, held her close, and whispered, "I'm fine, but we need to move, and we'll need to do it quickly." Hatch nodded to Corbin. "We're leaving now."

"Trouble, huh?" Corbin was already on his feet and packing up.

"Go pack up your things," he told Millie, and she quickly headed into the bedroom to comply.

"Isn't there always trouble?" Hatch asked Corbin, then quickly relayed what happened with Aman and the stranger.

Corbin's eyebrows shot up. "Interesting," he murmured. "I don't suppose you got any information out of them."

He shook his head. "Not much, but I did grab both of their cell phones."

"Oh, that's great. So it wasn't all for nothing." Corbin's gaze brightened.

Hatch tossed the cell phones to Corbin.

"We won't get out of the country," she called from the bedroom, then came out, looking over at Hatch, her expression worried. "Will we?"

"Not that fast, no," he replied, "but we definitely have to change locations. I've asked for a safe house," he murmured. "All packed up?"

Within seconds, she stood by the door, stunned, looking at all their personal belongings gathered beside her. The suite was all packed up; the leftover food had been tossed into the trash. "If I knew we would toss it—"

"Don't worry about it. We'll order more food," Hatch whispered. Soon they were outside.

She sniffed the cool air. "Such a hot mugginess here even when cloudy, even at this hour."

"I think it's the precursor to a rainstorm, but regardless we need to move fast. We'll have visitors soon."

"Did you leave somebody behind?"

"Nobody who'll talk." She pinched her lips together and just stared at him. He placed a finger against her lips, "It was necessary."

"You had to kill him?"

"One, yes, but he killed the other guy, Aman. I'll explain later." And, with that, he wrapped an arm around her shoulder, tugged her up close. "Stay with me, and let's be quiet."

Corbin went ahead, and they quickly followed. Corbin checked his phone a couple times, as if looking for instructions or directions, and, before she knew it, they were up against a building in a dark alleyway.

As Corbin stepped into the building, she hesitated. Hatch looked at her and whispered, "Safe house. Remember?"

"Scary, sketchy, dark cave. Remember?"

He nodded. "Trust me." He didn't really give her an option and just tugged her forward.

She wanted to protest, but there wasn't any protesting to be done. It was this or nothing, as far as they were concerned. She stepped in behind Corbin, and they were in a large room, with four bunk beds. She turned around and looked at Hatch. "Nobody knows we're here?"

Hatch immediately shook his head. "Not unless we were followed."

"Is that a possibility?" she asked.

"Isn't it always a possibility?"

"I'll go keep an eye out." Corbin dropped his load and stepped back outside again. As he walked past, he handed the phones back to Hatch. "Take a look at these while I'm gone," he muttered.

She sat on the bottom bunk closest to her and whispered, "What the hell happened over there?"

He quickly explained, while she stared at him in shock. "He killed his own friend?"

"I don't know about *friend*. Maybe somebody was keeping an eye on Aman or possibly somebody was sent to kill him. It may have been somebody in cahoots with Aman who refused to share the spoils. I don't know. The unknown guy would have killed me but stabbed his buddy instead, and I turned around and snapped his neck, without meaning to."

"Wow, the cops will really love you."

"No, they sure won't," he noted. "I highly suspect neither of those two were model citizens, and, even though it's a mess for the local authorities, they definitely won't love me, … if they find out that I was even there."

She snorted. "Spies are everywhere. Remember. Did you

get a picture of the other one?"

"I did," he confirmed. "I took pictures of both before I left."

He held up his phone, and she stared at it. "He seems vaguely familiar, but I'm not sure if he was part of my kidnapping or not."

"I wouldn't be at all surprised if he was."

When she looked at the photo again, she shifted in the light. "You know what? I think this was the second guard, the one who was more like the boss's assistant. It's just a really crappy photo."

"Well, he'll never get any better photos now," Hatch murmured.

She nodded slowly. "And I know I shouldn't be happy about that, but I find myself incapable of feeling sad that this asshole and Aman are dead."

"I get it." He sat down and brought out his laptop, then started typing away.

She stared at him. "What are you doing?"

"Arranging flights out of here," he murmured. "We might have to do a circuitous route though."

"Yeah, well, I'm not too into a circuitous route," she stated. "I'd like to get back to England as fast as possible."

"What about our forty-eight hours?" he asked. "I figured you would give us guff over leaving early."

"No, not if you were attacked here too," she explained. "And now that you've brought up my father's storage locker, I'm pretty sure that's where the boss would have gone."

"If he'd had any way to trace the locker's location, I'm sure he would have left immediately," he murmured. "But we don't know that he did, do we?"

"No, but I also don't know if they might have beaten

that information out of my father," she added. "And I don't know what further information taking his phone might have given them."

"Probably opened up a whole network of other avenues for the kidnapper," he murmured. "Think about it. That's one of the reasons I grabbed these cell phones before I left your two dead guards. Because we all do so much on our phones now, right?"

"We sure do."

He sat back, looked at her. "Did you get any sleep while I was gone?"

She snorted. "No, absolutely not. And I'm feeling way too wired to sleep now."

"Of course," he agreed. "When you experience a kidnapping like that, it's not exactly an easy thing to let go of."

"No," she whispered, "it's not. And I would just as soon have this all over with before I sleep again."

"We won't get that far," he noted. "We'll be here for a few hours for sure, so you need to get whatever sleep you can. Once we start traveling, it'll be a whole different story."

"Can we catch flights anywhere? That would be way faster."

"I've got our team working on that," he murmured. "Let's give them a chance to figure out what they can come up with."

She nodded and sat glued to her seat, clearly tense.

He walked over and sat down beside her. "You know it's not good to be so keyed up. You've got to relax."

"Sure." She stared at him. "You just killed a man. Once the cops find him, don't you think they'll be after you?"

"They might be," he admitted, "but first, they'll have to figure out who might have killed whom."

"Is it possible that it looked like they killed each other?"

"Quite possible." Hatch nodded. "The way the bodies were left, it was obvious that somebody from the ground might have kicked up, and, if he'd done that in the process of the knife going at him, it would have taken him down and out."

"Well, that would be an easy answer, but I doubt that it will end up being that simple," she muttered.

He smiled at her. "Believe me. In this case, that is not our problem."

"Unless you get picked up in the meantime."

"Which I'm trying not to do." He gave her half a smile. At that, his phone buzzed. He looked at it, nodded. "Don't unpack."

"Yeah? When are we leaving?"

"In an hour—or less," he stated. "They're sending a vehicle to pick us up."

She stared at him. "We can get out of here in less than an hour?"

"Yep," he stated. "Not necessarily as far away as we want to go, but we'll get out of the city at least."

"Where to?"

He smiled. "Not where you're expecting, but we can arrange further transport after this. The priority right now is to get ourselves out of here."

"Agreed. As long as we're out of Egypt, I'll be happy, I guess."

"Any plans to come back?"

She snorted. "After all this? Hell, no."

"Good. And, if the Egyptian government thinks you're associated with any of this, chances are you won't be allowed to come back anyway."

She winced at that. "That would hurt, as I do have an awful lot of history here. But, for the moment, I'm okay to do whatever needs to be done to put this to rest."

"It's more than just putting it to rest. It's still about keeping you safe and making sure the boss is caught and that you aren't subjected to his form of interrogation again."

"He didn't really interrogate me," she replied, for the sake of clarity.

"I know, but your father certainly was."

She winced at that. "And now that you've taken out one of his henchmen …"

"Or maybe the boss sent his assistant to take Aman out anyway," he muttered.

"Well, that would be a case of no honor among thieves."

"Which is very common." Hatch nodded. "There is never any honor among thieves. Especially when the spoils come to be divided or until somebody decides you are a liability," he explained, "and it's straight downhill from there."

She shook her head at that. "How do these people live with themselves?"

Hatch smiled. "When you think about it, they're doing what they think is normal, and they always think consequences won't ever happen to them. Although I have seen cases—where one person was to be taken out because the boss didn't like something they'd done—yet the targeted person took out the boss before it got to that point." Hatch quickly sent off a text, which she presumed was to Corbin outside.

"Does he need to grab his things?"

Hatch shook his head. "I'll grab everything that's here as we head out."

She nodded. "But it's still an hour away, right?"

He looked at his watch. "Nope, forty minutes. Or less. Let's just say, our plans are very fluid at the moment. Subject to change."

She sighed, got up, and went to the bathroom. She washed her hands and face, trying not to fuss about having no soap to really get them clean. She stepped back out again. "I won't sleep now. Any chance of us getting a nap wherever we go next?"

He smiled. "Maybe, but no guarantees."

"You're being very cryptic."

"I'm not trying to be, but I'm also trusting that wherever we're going is someplace that we need to be."

"Do you know where we're going?"

"Roughly, yes." Hatch nodded. "I'm just not sure how long we'll be there. It could be just for an hour or two. We'll be doing a series of helicopter runs, I think." She stared at him. He shrugged. "Don't worry about it."

"*Sure*, don't think about it. *Right*. That's not so easy, if you're me."

"I know," he murmured, "but, right now, the biggest thing is that we get out of here safely."

The knot in her stomach tightened up. She felt as if certain nerves were stretched to the breaking point.

Finally he looked at her, then smiled. "It's time. Come on. Let's go."

"Now?" she asked. "Is it time already?"

"Yes, believe it or not, it is."

She hesitated, then bounced to her feet, snatched up her bags. "Ready."

At that point, Corbin stepped inside to gather his bags, then looked over at Hatch. The two men shared a nod. With the rest of their gear in hand, they ushered her out ahead of them.

"Sure wish I knew we were going somewhere safe."

"You'll be a guest of the United States government."

She snorted at that. "Yet you said it wouldn't be for very long."

"Nope. Not very long at all." As they walked outside, a vehicle pulled up in front of them, and they were quickly ushered into the back seat, and it took off.

"Where are we going?" she asked, in a low voice, staring at the driver.

Hatch reached over, placed a finger against her lips, and whispered, "Don't talk." She stared at him mutely and sagged in her spot. She didn't have long to wait to get an answer. They were taken to a clearing, right next to a huge military helicopter.

Not what she thought of when she had heard the word "helicopter."

She shook her head, as they were ushered on board and very quickly lifted off. Once up, she couldn't hear anything because the noise was almost painfully loud. She watched in amazement as Cairo, Egypt, disappeared beneath her, and, all of a sudden, they were heading overseas.

As the water gleamed below them, she felt a mixture of hope and fear. She didn't know where they were headed, but she was relieved enough to focus on worrying about their destination. When they came down atop a huge destroyer, she gasped in shock. But they were quickly taken off the helicopter and ushered inside the warship and down a series of metal stairs and into a small room.

When she got into the room, Hatch pointed at the bunks, then turned and said something to the navy man outside. Then the door closed quietly on them. She looked at

Hatch in shock. "Good God."

"We're waiting for orders," he explained. "I doubt that we'll be here very long."

"No, most likely not," she agreed, "and I can't even believe we're here."

"It's only one of many legs on this trip," he added, "but we will get you to London soon."

And, true to his word, while she sat here waiting, Hatch had several communications back and forth, but nothing that ever included her. At this point she didn't even care about that; she just wanted their escape to be over. Several hours later they were taken by helicopter to another destroyer, where they waited for another few hours. She was able to nap there, and, before she knew it, Hatch was waking her up.

"Rise and shine. Time to go."

Still waking up, she couldn't place her situation right away. She stared at him, yet moved without a single question. This time they landed at an airport and, within twenty minutes, were loaded onto a small plane, with her seated on one side and him on the other, with an aisle between them. Each had two seats allotted, which made sleeping midflight a little comfier.

"It's morning?" she asked.

Hatch nodded, smiling.

"Where are we going now?" she whispered.

"England." Hatch smiled.

She sagged with relief. "Well, thank God for that."

"We're not out of danger yet," he murmured.

"No, I can imagine. Until we get in and clear customs …" She immediately thought about her passport and scrambled to find it.

He held it up in his hand, holding all three of their passports. "Don't worry. I've kept them all handy."

"Well, good," she replied. "It wasn't even at the top of my thoughts."

"Just rest for now," he said.

She looked at him in surprise. "Can I?" And then realized that it was just them on the plane, all but for the crew. "How did you guys commandeer this?"

"Again … I don't even know." Hatch smiled. "All kinds of equipment are available for our use, and we submit our needs, and someone figures it all out."

She didn't say anything, just leaned back and closed her eyes, wishing that the knot in her stomach would ease. But until they landed and cleared the airport, she wouldn't be calm enough for any of that. Neither could she sleep. She tossed and turned and wrestled against the oncoming darkness, and, just when she was starting to sleep, her eyes would pop open again. She cried out in a low tone.

He immediately looked over at her. "Can't sleep?"

She shook her head. "Every time I try, I keep getting jerked awake."

He immediately walked over and sat down beside her. He lifted the armrest, so it wasn't between them, then tucked her up against his chest. "Now, get some rest."

She looked at him. "I can't keep doing this."

"Why not? It's hardly an issue, at least right now. Besides, I'm on the same plane, doing nothing else, and you need to sleep."

"I won't fall asleep just because you order me to," she argued. But, when she woke several hours later, she realized she had done exactly that. She opened her eyes and stared for a moment. "Wow, you're better than a nightcap."

He burst out laughing. "Well, I'm glad to hear that." He

smiled. "Are you feeling better?"

She sat up and stretched her arms over her shoulders. Corbin sat across from them, sleeping gently. "Did you get any sleep?" she asked Hatch, immediately looking at him in worry.

"I took the first watch," he stated.

She snorted. "It's hardly a watch. We are up in the air, after all."

He grinned. "It becomes a habit after a while. One sleeps. The other one stays awake," he murmured. "It's all good."

She muttered, "I don't know about *all good*, but this still feels very much like a nightmare that just won't end."

"And yet, in just another couple hours, we'll be in London."

"Well, in that case, I wish we had food here."

"There is food. What would you like?" He opened up a small fridge nearby, where he pulled out an assortment of sandwiches and other snacks.

"I'll take anything," she admitted. "I can't believe how hungry I am all the time. And sleepy. And I know. ... I know." She held up a hand. "You'll say it's still a reaction to the trauma and shit."

"It's adrenaline. It's stress. It's grief. It's all kinds of things," he noted. "Besides, food is important for nourishment. And it also keeps up your energy."

"It seems like my energy is always flagging."

"Well, hopefully it won't be like that for much longer."

"Have you had any updates?"

"A few." Hatch nodded. "So far not any news on the two guards' bodies."

She nodded, snatched up the closest sandwich, and started eating.

THERE HADN'T BEEN any word on the bodies being found, which both worried and intrigued Hatch. Was somebody else involved in this who would dispose of the bodies or was that just an area of town where nobody expected anybody to show up for a while? If that were the case, it would take however long until somebody decided to check up on these men. Maybe not until the odor was an issue worth checking on. And, even then, Hatch wasn't sure many people would care about Aman, especially with his bad reputation.

Hatch had asked Killian several times if there'd been any updates, but always it was a no—not just a no but a big no. Also the Egyptian government hadn't had any clue about their quick exit from the country. Killian said that they would deal with it afterward. The first thing had been to get them out safely.

Even now, Killian was asking for answers as to what was in the locker. Hatch had said that they would update the team as soon as they got to England, stating that Millie didn't know what was in it. Killian had expressed a bit of doubt about that, but Hatch understood that. It was expected in a sense. The relationship between her and her father was strained at best. And now she was already dealing with guilt and an overwhelming sense of loss.

And learning the true cause of her mother's death had just added to Millie's pain. When he explained that to Killian, there had been no arguments from Killian's side. They all had to deal with people in traumatic situations, and sometimes there were just no good answers. Not at first.

Time would tell.

Mostly there were no answers initially, let alone good ones.

Hatch picked up a sandwich and ate it slowly. He thought Millie's sleeping pattern was definitely odd. He could understand it to some degree, but, at the same time, she might have trouble breaking it. He was okay if she didn't break it either. He'd be more than happy to have her sleep in his arms for the rest of eternity, but he wasn't about to share that just yet, of course. It sounded a little bit too much like the whole matchmaking thing going on with the rest of the Mavericks.

Hatch had been joking with Corbin about it at the very beginning of this op, and, sure enough, it seemed like it was potentially happening right under Hatch's nose. And he couldn't be happier. As far as whether or not she was a good fit for him, all he could think about was the way she'd handled herself, which he respected, and the attraction had been instant between them. Hatch knew Corbin had already seen it, but thankfully he hadn't commented on it, at least not to Hatch. It was one of those things that one really didn't want to have brought up until the relationship was a little further down the line.

"Penny for your thoughts," she said.

He looked over at her, smiled. "Not worth it."

"Are you kidding?" she asked. "Everything that you've got to say is always so intelligent and on target. It's obviously worth it." He looked at her in surprise. She shrugged. "I have to admit that I have felt fairly intimidated around you two."

"Well, that was not our intention," he stated immediately.

"No, I'm sure it wasn't," she murmured, "but it's a

throwback. My father was very much a person who you didn't want to disagree with or voice an opinion that differed from his own."

"Sounds like the old guard," he noted, "where women were meant to be seen and not to be heard."

"Yeah, that was him," she admitted. "Honestly I don't know how my mother stood him."

"Maybe that's why they spent as much time apart as they did," he commented.

"It's quite possible," she agreed. "It took me a lot of time to develop a thick skin with him. Even after that I still didn't do so well with him."

"And yet I think you did just fine," he murmured.

She smiled. He reached out, offering her a second sandwich. She hesitated and then shrugged. "Sure, though it seems that all I do around you is eat and sleep."

"I was just thinking about your sleeping habit," he noted.

"Yeah, I'm so sorry about that," she murmured. "It feels very strange to have this problem."

"It's not a problem and nothing to be ashamed of," he stated firmly. "I was just thinking about the fact that it was comfortable. That, in a way, it may be too comfortable."

"Meaning?" she asked him.

"Meaning, I like the feel of you in my arms," he stated.

She flashed a charming smile and her dimples at him. "Wow. Does that mean you're flirting with me?"

"I'm not sure that *flirting* is exactly the right word," he replied, "but it's definitely in the neighborhood."

"That's even better," she murmured. "I was thinking about how natural it's been and how very unusual it is for me to be comfortable around a man. But I think it comes back to trust and to the fact that I feel safe in your arms. And that's not a good thing either."

"Why is it not a good thing?" he asked in astonishment.

She flashed her smile again, but this time he didn't think it was with joy. "I just—that came out wrong," she stated. "I just meant that becoming dependent on you for something like that isn't a good thing."

"I can see how you would feel that way," he replied, "but it just goes back to what I said."

She nodded. "I really appreciate that you're trying to make me feel better."

"I'm not trying to make you feel better." Hatch shook his head. "It's the truth. I would really like it if we had lives that could intersect at some point in time. I would love it if we could get to know each other a little more."

She stared at him, and then she smiled a genuine smile, with some serious depth to it. "I'd really like that too," she said softly. "My life has been such a nightmare for a long time now, but that would be a return to something normal that I would really enjoy."

"Good. We'll see how we can make that happen."

"Yeah, and how would we do that?" she asked. "I don't even know where I'll be."

"Well, you're from the US, right?"

"Yes. And, yes, I'm returning there, and I presume you are from there also."

"Yes, I'm based out of California. What about you?"

She stared at him. "Well, I was in New York, but I haven't been there for a very long time. So, as much as I am an American, I don't really have a home base right now."

"You got anything against California?" he asked instantly.

She looked at him to see if he was serious, then burst into laughter. "Okay, so that might be getting a little pushy."

He grinned. "Are you sure?" he asked. "Because it makes an awful lot of sense to me."

"Well, I mean, in a way, … yes, it does," she stammered, "because you're the one who has a job. I, on the other hand, appear to be an unemployed bum." It was his turn to stare at her, and she laughed. "I was working on digs, but apparently I don't have any place to go to work now."

He smiled. "Do you have any of your father's stuff to wrap up?"

"Probably way too much of it actually." She winced. "When I think about it, I'll have all those reports and grants to deal with—and all kinds of other paperwork. I'm not too sure how I'm even supposed to bring it to an end."

"Well, we'll leave that until we get there. How about that?"

"I know I won't be allowed to go back and finish anything at his pending digs."

"No, but you probably will deal with some of the related paperwork."

"Maybe," she murmured. "It just seems like he …" Then she stopped, shook her head. "That's a really shitty thing to think."

"What? That he dumped it all on you?"

"Yeah," she agreed. "He died, so technically he didn't mean to dump anything on me. It was just … the circumstances."

"Keep that thought in mind." As he watched, he saw her sniffle a couple times. He immediately shifted, so he was closer. "I know this is really hard. And it will probably keep hitting you wrong in many ways for a long time to come. No easy way to deal with a loss like this, especially given the way it happened."

She nodded. "Every time I close my eyes, I always see that damn dirt tomb."

He nodded. "I'm not at all sure that you were intended to get out of there."

"No, I don't know if I was or not," she noted. "He didn't say anything, did he? Aman, I mean."

Hatch shook his head. "No, he didn't acknowledge that. The point is, he didn't deny that he was there or that he had something to do with it, but he seemed unsurprised that we knew about the foreman's death. He seemed unsurprised to hear that we were looking for you, and he seemed unsurprised that we knew your father was dead."

"Well, that's interesting," she murmured. "But then my father may have intentionally been dumped somewhere that he would likely be found. It would be nice to have his body to take home."

"The team will keep an eye out for any news on it. Don't worry. The US government is involved."

"Not sure that's a good thing," she noted. "To me, it seems so often that the governments are more headaches than they're worth."

"More often than not, that's exactly what they are," he agreed, "but, in this case, we have different governments involved."

"Right. You seem to have a lot of faith in yours."

"I have faith in the group I work with," he clarified, "not so much about the government suits. They tend to come and go."

"Oh, isn't that the truth," she agreed. "Sometimes it's a good thing, and sometimes it's a mess."

"Exactly," he murmured.

She looked down at the half sandwich she had left. "I don't think I can eat this." He held out his hand; she looked at it. "Do you want it?" He took the sandwich and downed it in a couple bites. "Well, okay. I guess there never are any leftovers with you guys, are there?"

"Nope, because we know the value of eating when there's time to eat. Sometimes we don't know when we'll get that next chance again."

She nodded, and then a yawn caught her by surprise. She stared at him, and he just grinned.

"Close your eyes, and get some rest."

"Yeah, we know how that works," she muttered.

"Well, you can always tuck up against my shoulder again."

She hesitated and then looked at him. "Would you mind terribly?"

"No, I won't mind," he replied softly. And, with that, she shifted closer and leaned her head against his shoulder, as he wrapped an arm around her and held her close. When he looked down a few minutes later, she was already out. Her chest rose and fell in a slow steady pattern.

He'd never met anybody who could sleep like that or who could go out so fast. Clearly something about her and him together was helping her to doze off without any trouble at all. When he looked over, Corbin was awake and studying the two of them. Hatch shrugged. "I don't know, man. I'm not exactly sure what's happening here."

"You may not be sure, but you're damn well looking forward to finding out."

He winced. "Is it that obvious?"

"Yes, and it should be," Corbin stated. "This is a good

thing. Remember?"

"Maybe, but she's still got some pretty hefty issues to deal with."

"We all do," Corbin murmured. "So why don't you have a nap yourself, and I'll wake you guys up when we have a few minutes to go."

And, with that, Hatch closed his eyes and drifted off to sleep himself.

CHAPTER 12

A GENTLE HAND on her shoulder woke her up. Millie bolted upright and stared, blinking like an owl. "Where are we?" She looked around in shock.

"We're still on the plane, but we're coming in for a landing."

She stared at him. "Where?"

"London," he replied. "It's a small private hangar though."

"Great. Will we have any trouble there?"

"I don't think so," he said gently. "Let's go."

And, with that, the plane was already on the ground and taxiing toward the buildings. She waited until they pulled up to the hangar, where the plane came to a stop. The men opened the doors, and she stepped out. "What about customs?"

"Paperwork's already been faxed through," he murmured.

"Wow."

Looking at her calmly, he added, "We do have some connections here."

"So … we don't have to go through customs?"

"No, not the way you traditionally would," he noted. "Don't worry. Cameras are here, and people will be checking to see that the passengers we listed got off the plane and that we didn't bring anybody extra." Hatch gave her a gentle smile.

"I think I like traveling this way," she noted. "It's much easier."

And, sure enough, they went through the hangar, out to the other side, where a vehicle waited for them. "I've never gone through customs or entered a country so easily."

"And again," he noted, "it wouldn't happen all the time, but right now that's what needed to happen."

"Where do we go from here?" she asked.

"We're heading to your father's locker."

She frowned. "Right." She groaned. "Back to business then?"

"In this business, we never stop working," Corbin stated. "And, in this case, this is a pretty important step."

She fell silent at that. She didn't want to think of this as *all* being business, but, of course, that's what it seemed like now. When she looked over at Hatch, she struggled, trying not to judge him for making her feel that way, because it wasn't his comment; it had been Corbin's.

Almost as if Hatch understood what she felt, he reached a hand quietly across the back seat and just held hers. She stared down at their intertwined hands and sighed. He gave her a gentle squeeze and didn't say a word. She realized that nothing had changed between them. It was just Corbin's way of reminding them that they had business to settle up and that everybody needed to be alert. She couldn't argue with that either.

Obviously it had been imperative to get the hell out of Egypt when they did, and even now she would be quite happy to never go back. And yet that was in direct conflict with what she'd already spent most of her life studying.

Maybe it was time for change.

The fact of the matter was, she didn't know how everything had gotten so ugly so quickly. She didn't know what she would feel like as soon as they got to the locker or even after this nightmare was over. Thinking about that, she asked, "May I borrow your laptop? I need to find the combo numbers to get in."

"Do you have them?" He looked over at her.

"I do, I just need to find them." She brought up her email on his laptop and searched through them until she found the combination. "It's here." She held up the screen for him.

He used his phone and took a photo of it. "Now we both have it, just in case. We always need to have a backup."

But as he stared at his screenshot for a long moment, she asked, "You just memorized it, didn't you?"

He smiled. "Just in case."

She swallowed at that. "*Just in case.* You've said that twice now. Are we expecting a reception committee at the locker or something?"

"Expecting? ... No. Anticipating? ... Most likely, yes," he replied.

"Crap. I really would like to never have to see the boss or any of those guys again."

"Well, the two guards from Egypt will no longer be involved because they're dead, and any henchmen you see now will be a whole new kettle of fish," he explained. "So don't trust anybody right out of the gate."

She stared at him. "I guess I wasn't even thinking along those lines."

"Well, we have to be ready for anything," he noted. "The boss who kidnapped you might expect to see you here, or he might be stunned to find out you're alive. There is even a possibility that he might not even be here. But, at the same time, it could be the boss's own boss or henchmen higher up the ladder. Or neither. Hell, it could be a totally different third player. We just need to be prepared for anything,"

"Wow, that's reassuring," she muttered. Then added under her breath, "Not."

He chuckled. "Remember. We've come this far. We won't ditch you now. We're planning on getting us all out of this alive."

She nodded slowly. "Well, you've certainly managed so far, and I appreciate that."

"Good." He smiled. "We can get through this. Just remember. We're handling it as best we can, with what intel we have, and we won't always get answers just because you want them."

"Oh, I understand that already." She gave a heavy sigh. "It would be nice, but, at least if we can get something," she added, "it would make me feel better." She noted they were coming into the district where she knew the locker was located. "Wow, we're already here."

"We've been driving for nearly thirty minutes," Corbin announced from the seat behind Hatch, "so it hasn't been all that fast."

"Feels like it," she replied immediately.

When they pulled up to park, Hatch looked at her. "Are you ready for this?"

"Hell no, I'm definitely not ready."

"I get that," he noted, "but unfortunately it's now or never."

HATCH HOPPED OUT of the vehicle and closed the car door behind him. He heard Millie's muffled protest, but it was best if she stayed behind with Corbin. Hatch quickly entered the combination into the lock. The fact that there was a lock meant nothing to him. There were all kinds of ways to get into these places.

It was also quite possible that they had been followed, although that wasn't terribly likely. He just didn't want Millie to get caught up in the same kidnapping scenario she'd been in before. He opened the door and then stepped inside the locker. He quickly moved through the storage locker area, full of crates, and noted right away that it was way bigger than the single 10'x10' allotment that he had expected to see. *This* was like a commercial warehouse.

He stopped in the center, listening, and, instead of silence, he heard a voice up ahead. But it wasn't talking to him. Then he heard a second voice. He quickly texted Corbin to let him know. As much as he would like Corbin to back him up, Hatch needed his partner to take care of Millie. And that would be his first priority.

Hatch slipped through the dark shadowy aisles, heading toward the voices. When he got there, he stopped just short of rounding the corner, where he would be seen. He heard the two men talking.

"Is all of this from Egypt?" one asked.

"I don't know," the other one replied. "We'll have to do an inventory."

"Are we expecting visitors?"

"No, at least I don't think so. Nobody knows about the locker, and Marcus is dead."

"What about the daughter?"

"She should be dead too," the second man stated.

The boss. The voices were not familiar to Hatch, and he desperately needed to see who was here. Yet he suspected that one of these would be the boss man from Egypt, but that didn't mean he was at the root of all this mess. Frankly anyone could be the source of this problem at this point.

"If all of this has been stolen, then nobody will have any history and nothing to track, right? That means, it's ours for the taking, but I'm not comfortable leaving it here. I want everything moved into a more secure location. Then we'll decide who to target and what kind of prices we're looking at. This will go to private collections only."

"It'll have to," the other guy said, "because, if anybody sees this, … recognizes any of these pieces, chances are …"

"I know," the first guy stated, "but, as long as all the players down the line have been taken out, we won't have to worry about it." There was silence, and he added, "You do know for a fact that they've all been taken out, don't you?"

"Yes," the boss confirmed. "I sent an assassin to take out my guard, and, apparently in the process, they took out each other."

"Well, that's perfect." He laughed. "I bet the police were confounded by that."

"I don't think they've even found the bodies. I sent somebody looking for proof of the job done, and he confirmed two bodies. He disposed of them for me, but then he disappeared as fast as possible, and he doesn't want to work for me anymore. It's too dangerous."

Definitely the boss man, Hatch thought, adding a mental match up of the description Millie had given of the man in the shadows who'd pulled the strings over her kidnapping.

Just need to figure out who the other guy is.

"Good, then we don't have to worry about him either."

"He doesn't know anything, so it's a perfect scenario."

"Well, that was lucky," he agreed.

The boss added, "Now all we need to do is make sure that nobody at this end has any clue about this locker."

"Well, we can get it emptied soon enough. That would secure this inventory."

"As far as I know, only the father was aware of this storage area."

"Well, there's always somebody else. Did you check his call history? Any emails?"

"Yes. All cleared."

"And the daughter?"

"She was left locked in a cave in the desert to die," the boss confirmed.

"Good," the stranger replied.

"Somebody will find her body in another few thousand years or so."

"Maybe, if that is truly the case," he noted.

"What do you mean?"

"Did your jailer confirm that she died?"

"No, he closed the door and walked away."

"Good," the stranger replied. "The less tracks, the better."

"And now that he's dead as well, and nobody's there to track him down, all the better."

"Exactly," the stranger agreed. "Okay then, seems like we're in the clear."

"Good. Let's make arrangements," the boss said. "We need a warehouse that is way the hell larger than this one, so we can sort the inventory while we're there, and we need to—" He stopped. "So, do we have to worry about anybody who did the shipping?"

"I don't believe so," the other man replied. "The contents were crated before everything was loaded, and, as you can see, most of this has not been unpacked. Nobody should know what is held inside."

"Right, so okay. … That makes sense. I'm just wondering if we need to keep a watch on this place to see if anybody else knows about it."

"Well, since we've found it," the stranger replied, "I've had men posted to watch it, and nobody has come or gone."

"Well, that's good," the boss agreed. "Okay, let's just make arrangements to get everything out of here as quickly as possible. Then we'll put a new lock back on it and leave it empty. Meanwhile we can also hire somebody to come set up security cameras," the boss added. "That way we'll see if anybody else is interested in this place. If so, … we'll take them out, just to be sure."

"That's fine," the stranger said. "Where do you want to set up the new warehouse?"

"Well, closer would be better, but not so close that anybody can track it back to us. We really don't want to be in the same area."

"No, of course not," he agreed.

"And we'll need a trucking company in to move it all."

"Yeah? How quickly can we make that happen?" the stranger asked.

"As soon as we settle on a location, so probably forty-eight hours at most," the boss estimated.

"Make it twenty-four. There are big warehouses over near the commercial line," he noted. "Let's pick one of those."

"Let me see what's available." The boss stepped off a few steps and started making phone calls.

Hatch took a chance and peered around the corner, studied the first man, getting a good visual on him, who even now was eyeing one of the open crates with a look of greed on his face.

The stranger muttered under his breath, "This stuff will bring us a fortune."

As Hatch watched, the boss man, who was supposedly making phone calls, lifted a sledgehammer and swung it hard, taking out his partner without any warning.

Hatch was in shock himself, but the stranger went down without a whimper. His head was clearly smashed open by the sledge, and now an ever-widening puddle of blood covered the packing material he had fallen on. The boss quickly bundled it all together, using plastic, packing paper, and duct tape.

Before long, a completely packaged mummy lay on the ground.

Hatch stared at it, wondering at the efficiency that went into something like that. He quickly backed away and, in the process, bumped into an aisle. Even then, as he tried to step back, something wobbled behind him.

The boss stopped immediately and searched in the darkness around him.

Quickly avoiding whatever it was that wobbled, Hatch shifted, moving as soundlessly as possible.

"Well, I don't know who you are," the boss man called out, his voice calm, "but I can tell you that you're never getting out of here. I don't like people spying on me."

Hatch didn't say anything but moved in the darkness and then crouched down low on one of the empty shelves.

The killer had a flashlight, and he moved swiftly through the warehouse, heading toward Hatch.

"I don't know who the hell you are," the boss yelled, his voice getting angrier and angrier, "or what you want, but you're just pissing me off."

Pissed off or not, no way the killing boss would let some interloper live when he found Hatch.

"I may not know you, but, but this? … This is my gig. Not yours. You hear me? It's all mine. It doesn't happen too often that you get a plum like this dropped into your lap. Besides, that other guy deserved to die. Do you have any idea how many men he had killed?" he snapped.

Hatch didn't say anything again, and he wasn't sure he had anything to say. The boss was obviously up for killing anybody who interfered in his life, so Hatch's lack of words wouldn't make a bit of difference to the boss man. Hatch waited until the guy came along on the far side, his flashlight sweeping through.

Then the boss started to swear. "Jesus Christ. I don't even know for a fact if somebody is in here." The flashlight moved with a rapid precision but didn't pick up anything.

Finally he calmed down and gave half a laugh. "Man, I'm losing it." He went back over to the body and gave it a hard kick. "Asshole," he muttered. "You have no idea how good it feels to know that you're dead as a doornail and won't be ordering me around anymore. Now …" he said to himself, "it is time for you to get the hell out of here."

At that, he walked over and hopped onto the forklift, then picked the body up using the forks, took it over to an open crate, and dumped in the mummified body. After that, he used a whole pile of packing material to cover it up. He added some packing beads, probably the ones that took away moisture to stop anything from molding on the inside, and then he picked up the lid and very securely put it on the top.

Hatch quickly noted exactly which crate it was, taking a picture of it, as the boss secured it shut. Then slowly Hatch stepped back. He was one more step away, when the boss turned and looked in Hatch's direction.

"Somebody *is* there," he stated with conviction; then, moving as fast as he could, he raced forward.

Hatch stepped against the shelving and waited until the boss came around the corner because this had to come to an end.

As soon as the boss appeared, Hatch screamed at the top of his voice.

The boss bolted sideways, and Hatch reached out with a hard right and knocked him down. At that, the boss jumped forward, and the fight was on. Unfortunately the boss seemed to be just about as much of a street fighter as Hatch was. They went several rounds, until a shot was fired over their heads.

Hatch immediately froze and stared at the boss man, who had a big grin on his face.

"Look at that," the boss crowed, pointing to the back door. "Good timing, Morris."

And, with that, both Corbin and Millie were pushed forward toward the light in the center. Hatch stepped back ever-so-slightly to see Morris, the newcomer, standing there, holding a gun on Corbin.

"Looks like I did some very efficient hiring after all," the boss man stated.

Hatch looked over at him. "What is killing your partner even worth?"

"A lot ..."

"You murdered your boss and stuck him in that crate over there. Does Morris know that he's next?"

"You did what?" Morris asked in shock. "Where's Henrique?"

"He's in that crate." Hatch pointed. "This guy killed him with a sledgehammer."

"No way," the boss man argued. "Henrique is my boss. I work for him."

Morris turned the gun on the boss, and things got intense. "Did you kill him?"

"Come on. Come on, Morris. You know it had to happen. We even talked about it."

"Like hell we talked about it," he spat. "You think I would double-cross my boss? I just hadn't had a chance to talk to him because we've been so damn busy."

"Yeah, well, you didn't warn him in time, so now he's gone. Decide quickly what you'll do about it," the killer sneered.

Not one moment of thinking lapsed, before Morris fired a bullet right into the killer's chest.

The killer stared in shock, as he went down in a pool of his own blood.

Corbin was already on Morris, even as Hatch ran toward Millie. Then Hatch heard Morris's gun firing again and again, and Corbin took a bullet in the shoulder. Hatch heard Millie shrieking in the distance, and then came a sudden hard crack. As Hatch neared Millie, she stood there, with a broken piece of pottery, standing over Morris, who now was on the floor.

Still woozy, Corbin dropped to the ground and checked Morris's pulse. "He's alive." He looked over at Hatch.

Hatch raced to Millie's side, noting her shocked look,

and took the piece of pottery from her hands. "It's okay. It's okay. You did good. Let it go now."

She stared at him. "My God. What the hell is going on here?"

"Well, an awful lot is going on," Hatch noted, "but I think, at the moment, we might have got down to finally figuring out the truth." He smiled at her, wrapped her up in his arms. "Not only did you do good"—he gave her a big smile—"you did great!"

She looked over at Corbin. "But he's been shot."

Corbin held up a hand. "It's nothing. Just a minor flesh wound." And he showed her. "I've had a lot worse."

She winced at the burn on his shoulder, then took in the implications of what he said. "My God." Then she turned into Hatch's embrace again, as his arms closed securely around her.

Hatch looked over at Corbin. "You okay?"

Corbin nodded. "Yeah, but we'll need to get a team in here pronto, and, like it or not, it's got to be MI6."

Hatch winced at that. "They're really not our friends at this point."

"I'm not sure we have any real friends in law enforcement around the world," Corbin replied, "but this is bigger than us."

"I know," Hatch agreed.

"I'll make the call," Corbin stated.

"Get yourself some medical attention too," Millie added, turning to look at Corbin.

"No," he argued, "not now. We'll need to talk to you about everything in here."

She nodded slowly. "I get that. I'm not happy at what I'm seeing, but trust me. I get it."

Hatch called out to Corbin, "Make the calls, and then we'll have a talk about whatever the hell is going on here."

She looked up at Hatch. "Are you okay?" She reached her hand to his swollen jaw. "You took a huge risk."

"Somebody had to," he said cheerfully. "I wouldn't let you deal with these guys."

"Did you know they were in here?"

"No, but I had to assume that they were or that they would be soon," he noted. "We had to prepare for that. Anything less would add even more risk of getting into even more trouble. I was uncomfortable without more intel to go on."

She nodded slowly, then she looked up at him. "Well, we're one step closer."

"We're multiple steps closer now," he confirmed.

She smiled, "I meant, … when this is all over, maybe having some time, … like, *together*. And maybe we can get to know each other better, like you said earlier."

He grinned. "We are definitely closer to that now too."

CHAPTER 13

MILLIE SIGHED. AS it was, it all took a whole lot longer than expected. MI6 arrived with somebody they called Jonas. They all spoke as if they knew each other well. Jonas didn't appear to be pleased to see the bodies, and, when he took note of the warehouse full of antiquities, he turned to study her intently.

"What do you know about this stockpile?" he asked her.

She shrugged. "I know this was my father's warehouse, but had never been inside here and didn't know what was being stored here."

"Are these stolen?"

"To the best of my knowledge, no," she replied, "but I haven't had a chance to even look to see what is here."

He nodded. "Well, I need you to look now."

She winced. "*Great,*" she murmured. "Any chance that you won't jump to conclusions and base it on appearances, without giving me a chance to find out if it is stolen or not?"

"I'd love to," he replied, "but, if you think that means you've got time to sort through all this, then the answer is no. Nothing goes in or out of this place without us recording it either."

She gave him a flat stare. "Meaning, now you think that I'll steal it?"

"I don't even know if it's stolen goods," he replied, "so

how could I think that? However, your attitude isn't helpful."

Immediately Hatch stepped up and said, "She's only just found out about this herself, so stop being such a hard-ass."

Jonas looked over at him and growled. "If you guys would stop filling my world with bodies, it might improve my mood immensely."

"Looks like neither of us are likely to get what we want," Hatch continued cheerfully.

"So you better stop bugging me."

At that, Hatch just rolled his eyes, as he walked toward her. "I don't know if you can even begin to identify anything here," he murmured, "but, if you can quickly see or identify what is or isn't stolen, that would help."

She nodded. "I'll take a look." That would be better than turning around and spitting back at this Jonas person. She understood that they were all used to these life-and-death scenarios, but she wasn't. What she'd been through these last few days had been traumatic and deadly, and it was all she could do to try to maintain some semblance of balance.

And the thought that Jonas wanted her to make a decision on all this stuff right now was crazy and nearly impossible. If only her father had left her some records of what was here. Then she stopped, walked back over to Hatch. "Have you seen any sign of an office here?"

He looked at her in surprise, turned around. "That would be a good thing to search for, wouldn't it?"

She nodded. "There has to be a manifest, a list of some kind. There's got to be a computer or something here."

"Okay." Hatch nodded. "I'll go take a look. You wander about and take a look."

And she did exactly that. She opened a few crates and determined that some of the stuff definitely hadn't come from Egypt. For all she knew, it came from various other dig sites. What she didn't know is why or how long her father had stockpiled these pieces.

She found no real dates on anything. Plenty of barcodes but not a whole lot else. She went to the dusty corners and found several other items that made her eyes pop.

Some of this stuff hadn't seen the light of day in decades, but that didn't mean that any of it was stolen. Although, if it came from other countries without the proper paperwork, then chances are it was. Had her mother known? And worse than that, had her mother been a part of this?

Millie had no real answers, when she heard Hatch calling out for her. She walked toward his voice. "What did you find?"

He held up some papers. "Found a computer, a manifest, and a set of books," he replied.

"Good," she murmured.

At that, Jonas said, "I'll take the books."

She glared at him. "You got a warrant?"

"I'll get one," he snapped, "and besides, you've got two bodies in here, so I have the upper hand. Any judge would grant my request in a minute."

Not a whole lot she could do to argue about that. "You don't get to have access to anything in here unless you can prove it is stolen."

He glared at her. "You don't get access to it until you can prove that it was your father's, legally and rightfully aboveboard."

"Well, if I get a chance to look at some of these manifests," she explained, "I can tell you more." She snatched the ledger from his hand, then walked over and sat down not too far away. At the front of the book, she immediately found a note addressed to her. With a shaking hand, she opened it.

Dear Millie, You know I love you, right?

"Yeah, sure," she muttered under her breath. At that, Hatch sat down beside her. He saw what she had open in front of her, but he didn't interfere and just let her read it.

The trouble is, just because I love you doesn't mean it was easy to try to reform my ways. While your mother was alive, she kept me in check, but, with her loss, it seemed like I reverted to what I have always been, which is a grave robber. I've always loved these artifacts and this evidence of the past and felt like no government gave a damn about it.

The bureaucrats were always about tourist dollars and capitalizing on some of these beautiful and absolutely incredible antiquities. Somebody needed to care about them, and somebody needed to look after these items and ensure that they didn't disappear into the black market. You have to understand that I'm not selling them, that I'm not giving them away. I've been preserving them for a time when the governments were ready to handle these treasures properly.

Unfortunately all I saw was that the governments were getting worse and worse, and the economy around me was getting worse and worse.

Some of what is here is from before your mother reformed me. And much of it is after she left us. I am sorry, but she was murdered, something that I don't know if you even know about. It was something I couldn't face because I felt like ultimately her death was caused by my grave-robbing work—something that she didn't know about from before. Somebody is after this hoard. Somebody found out about it, which was my fault, through my overuse of liquid gold, … liquid courage. At some point, I became a hunted man. I thought I was fine, safe in Egypt, doing the work I've always done. But, once he found me, then there was really no hiding anymore.

My end was written in stone the moment I had spoken. I didn't know how to get out of it. I didn't know what to do about it, but I figured that, sure enough, I would be in this predicament at one time or another. I've sent this letter to a friend, who has put it inside the ledger for you to find. He was already elderly and dying, having spent a lifetime as my assistant over the years, mostly doing this for the same reasons as I do, … the love of the actual history involved.

He had nothing to do with the import-export of any of this collection. He doesn't even know where this inventory came from, and, lucky for me, he didn't ask me any questions. But I've asked him to put this with the rest of the products, knowing that you will be the one who is left to deal with what I've amassed here, for all the world to see.

She lifted her head and stared at Hatch. "He sent this letter back, probably from Egypt, as if knowing he was already in trouble and would get kidnapped or killed."

Hatch nodded. "I read a little over your shoulder. I'm sorry for you, but it sounds like he already knew that his days were numbered."

"Apparently he got drunk and talked one time too many."

At that, Hatch winced. "That will do it."

"He sent this letter back to a friend, who's always accepted the receipt of the deliveries and has done the archiving. Somebody who absolutely loves these finds and didn't ask any questions. He kept his solid reputation and didn't have anything to do with the illegal aspects of it."

"Good," Hatch noted, pointing at Jonas, on his phone, hanging nearby. "It sounds like Jonas just found out that the person who's been seen here last has just died of cancer a week ago."

"In a way, that's nice," she noted. "At least he didn't find out what happened to my father."

"Right."

She murmured, "He says he left detailed records."

"Good." Hatch nodded. "Maybe with that, we'll decide what to do with everything."

She winced. "Chances are, the pieces will all need to be returned to the countries from which they came. My father had this love-hate relationship with governments, and the heart of a preservationist allowed him to justify taking everything," she whispered. "God, it's not exactly the legacy I think he thought he was leaving behind."

"When we start dabbling in illegal markets, this kind of legacy is what we leave behind," he muttered.

"He never sold anything, never gave anything away," she corrected him quickly. "He just stored it all, hoping that, at some point in time, somebody in the world would care a little more than the current governments."

Hatch stared at her. "So he was that naïve?"

"He does mention that all he saw was the world getting worse. While he had hoped it would get better, it just got uglier."

He nodded. "And I can't see that it'll change anytime soon."

"I know," she whispered. She slowly folded the letter. "Do you think it's a problem if I keep this?"

"No, I don't think so, but you'll have to let Jonas see it—or at least make a copy of it. I know that Jonas will try and confiscate everything here."

"Only if he wants the job and the expense of sorting out what goes to which country," she noted quietly. "Otherwise that would be the job I would take on for the next however long it takes."

"Well, in that case, I suggest you work alongside him, so you can undo or redo or however you want to refer to fixing your father's legacy."

At that, Jonas spoke up. "I'd like to see the letter and get a copy of it."

She looked up, tears still in her eyes, and nodded slowly. "I don't see that as a problem, but I want to make sure that all this inventory goes back where it belongs."

Jonas nodded. "I'm sure we can come to an agreement over that."

"I hope so." She nodded. "I'd like to think that my father left behind more than just this mess as his life's work. He wasn't always like this," she explained.

"I know that." Jonas nodded. "He has always been very respected within his field."

"He didn't steal it in order to sell it for personal gain," she added. "He honestly didn't believe the governments were doing justice by these beautiful pieces left behind by the generations before. In his own misguided way, he was just trying to safeguard it all."

At that, Jonas winced. "You know it'll be hard to convince everybody of that truth."

"Well, in that case"—she looked down at the letter—"maybe the letter needs to stay with the archives. You can have a copy, but we'll share a copy of the letter with each government, so everybody can thoroughly understand how my father felt about the way these bureaucrats treated these artifacts that he cared so much about. It will help people to understand the mind-set that drove him to hoard what he thought would become something the world would only exploit and would not cherish and protect."

Jonas nodded slowly. "But you do realize it will also show people what happened to him."

She nodded. "I know, and history won't be kind, but I think it's important that the truth be told."

"I agree," Hatch said. "I'm really proud of you for going that route."

She sniffled slightly. "But I do want to be a part of sending these things wherever they need to go."

Jonas nodded. "I think we can make that happen."

She looked over at Hatch. "Do we need to stay here right now?"

"Not only do we *not* need to stay here," he said, eyeing Jonas, "but they probably don't want us here while they deal with the forensics."

She nodded and slowly stood, keeping the letter clutched to her. When Hatch reached out a hand for it, she looked at him in surprise.

"Let me take a photo of it."

She nodded. They flattened the letter so Hatch could take a photo to send to Jonas. "Just as a point of good faith," he explained.

Jonas nodded and turned toward her. "I'm sorry."

Her hand went to her heart, then she nodded. "Thank you for that." And she let Hatch lead her outside. Once in the bright sun, she whispered, "Where do we go from here?"

"To a hotel," he replied. "There we can get a shower and a chance to clean up, after a very rough few days."

"You think?" she asked. "I mean, I get it in the sense that we finally have some answers, but it's devastating to know that those answers are the ones that I was desperately hoping not to get."

"I know," he whispered.

She noted a vehicle driving toward them. "Who's that?"

"Corbin," Hatch replied.

She snorted. "You two are always together, aren't you?"

"No, not always," he said, "but we've been friends for a very long time."

"Then you are blessed," she noted. "Living the lifestyle that I've chosen, I haven't had much chance to make friendships like that."

"I think that's why Corbin and I are as close as we are because we both live that lifestyle. We connected, and, through our work, we stay connected." He smiled.

They got into the vehicle with Corbin, and he looked over at them both. "You guys okay?"

"Well, I will be," she replied, "but I don't expect that to be today." She pointed at his shoulder. "Are you okay?"

"One of Jonas's guys patched me up." He gave a somber nod. "Let's get to a hotel."

It wasn't very long before they pulled up to the front entrance, and they got out. She looked at Corbin expectantly. "Are you coming in?"

"Yeah, we've all got rooms up there," he replied. "I'll go park around back." And, as soon as Hatch and Millie exited the vehicle, he drove off.

She headed to the reception desk, but then she stopped and looked at Hatch. "Do we need to check in?"

He shook his head. "No, we don't."

At the elevator, he hit the call button and wrapped an arm around her shoulder. "We have our rooms reserved already."

She nodded, then stepped inside the elevator, thankful that it was empty. She stayed within the circle of his arms. "Is it over?" she asked in a small voice.

"Absolutely, it's over," he said. The elevator stopped on the third floor. He stepped out and led her to a room, then pulled a key from his pocket.

"Did Corbin give that to you?"

"Yep." Hatch then unlocked the door and stepped inside.

She looked around. "Is Corbin staying with us?"

"Nope, he's got the room next door." Hatch pointed to the connecting door.

"Oh, good." She then stopped at the single king-size bed in the room and turned to look at him.

He smiled. "I wasn't sure if you'd sleep well on your own."

She rolled her eyes at that. "God, I'm pathetic, aren't I?"

"Not at all." Hatch walked forward, then gently pulled her into his arms and held her.

She wrapped her arms around him. "It's so foolish, but I'll certainly have to get used to it sometime."

"Nobody said you had to do it today though. It's easier to face something like that when you're feeling a whole lot more balanced than you are right now."

"Maybe," she murmured, "but it also feels foolish."

He chuckled. "I don't think so. Now, do you want to rest or do you want to go out for a meal? It's your choice. So what would you like to do?"

She lifted her head. "Oh my, … can we go out for a nice meal?"

"Absolutely," he said. "Do you want to shower first?"

She nodded immediately. "Definitely. Is Corbin joining us for dinner?"

"I can ask him." At the look on her face, he added, "Unless you don't want him to come."

She smiled at him, as she suggested, "Well, we could call it a date, but only if we go together without him."

Hatch laughed. "You know what? I don't think he'd have a problem with that."

"Are you sure?"

He nodded. "Believe me. Corbin understands."

"I'm not even sure I understand." Millie shook her head. "So I don't know how he could."

"You'd be surprised. He's pretty astute."

"Maybe," she muttered. "Still, it feels strange, and I probably shouldn't even have said anything about it."

"Too late now," Hatch stated. "Go have a shower and get changed. Meanwhile I'll talk to him when he comes up."

She nodded and dashed into the bathroom, more embarrassed than she expected to be. After she had a shower and soaked her head several times with shampoo and conditioner, she stepped out and dried off. Going through her clothing, she didn't have a whole lot of choices, but she did have a couple nice pieces. No dresses by any means, but she chose a nice top and some decent slacks. With that on, she stepped out into the room to find Hatch sitting there, waiting for her. "Hey, are you ready?" she asked.

He nodded. "As long as I can go like I am."

"Right. Sorry, just because I changed doesn't mean you have to."

He smiled, looked at her. "You look absolutely lovely."

She laughed. "Believe me. I don't feel that way. I feel a bit more like overdone toast with a thin bit of butter on top."

"So, just on the edge of crumbling?"

"Something like that," she muttered, walking over to stand in front of him. "What about Corbin?"

"He's not even free," he explained. "He's meeting up with Jonas again."

"Good. So where are we going?"

"A nice restaurant is just around the corner," he suggested, "as long as you're okay with Indian food."

"Totally okay with it," she said. "In fact, I love Indian food." And that's what they did. For the first time she remembered what it was to laugh and to smile and to relax.

Halfway through dinner, he noted, "I'm seeing a completely different side of you tonight."

"Yeah, I don't know if it's a good sign or not." She smiled at him. "But it feels great to unwind."

He nodded. "There is a certain amount of relief in just having made it this far, isn't there?"

"Absolutely," she agreed, "and I keep hoping that this will be the end of it."

"It is. Absolutely it is." Then he hesitated.

"What?" she asked, sensing a change in him.

"While you were in the shower, I got a message, saying that a body was found out in the desert."

She immediately froze. "Is it my father?"

"I don't know yet," he stated, "but there is a chance. For

now, let's just say it's in rough shape but a tentative match."

She stopped for a moment, thought about it. "Can you, … can we know for sure? It would be good to get him home."

"I would hope so," he said. "Let's see if we can get a positive ID, and then, if it's him, we'll make arrangements."

She smiled. "Are you heading back to the US right away?" she asked, squinting at him from under her lashes.

"Not necessarily," he replied. "Why?"

She shrugged. "I'm just not quite ready to say … goodbye."

"Good, because I'm not ready to say goodbye at all, even if I do have to go back."

She stopped, considering his words. "I guess that's the thing, isn't it? We're in a global world now."

"Absolutely. I can stay in England for a while. Considering we still potentially have your father's body to deal with, plus all this mess going on here with the inventory," he said, "that might not be a bad idea. I'll have to talk to my team and see just what I'm supposed to do at this point."

"Good. I like the idea of you staying around."

"I'll see if I can make it happen, without causing too much stress for anybody," he explained. "For all I know, it's a non-issue."

"I like the sound of that too." She laughed. "It seems like we haven't really had a chance to get to know each other, outside of all the drama."

"No, we haven't, but this evening is going a long way to reinforce what I already knew."

"And what's that?" She put down her fork and pushed away her empty plate.

"That I really like who you are," he admitted, "and I

really respect what you've been through and how you held up and, … I really like the person, that lovely little imp, who's inside."

She laughed. "That imp hasn't had a chance to show up in a very long time."

"Well, we'll work on that," he said. "I've seen bits and pieces of it, just little tiny peeks of it coming through sometimes." He smiled. "I'm hoping we can coax it out more often."

"Maybe." She paused, looked at him. "It seems like it's been a long time."

"And that will ease up now," he noted.

Such assurance was in his voice that she was surprised. "Are you sure about that?"

"I'm absolutely positive." He looked at her empty dinner plate. "Do you want some dessert?"

She shook her head. "Nope. Do you know what I want?"

"What's that?" he asked.

She leaned forward. "I want to go home and screw your brains out."

He stared, and she flashed him a bright smile. "I guess it wasn't the appropriate thing to say, huh?"

"Oh, it was the right thing to say," he replied in a strangled voice. "But your timing sucks because we still have to get all the way back to the hotel."

She burst out laughing. "But it's not that far away."

"And we'll get there in double-time." He stood and asked for the bill. He swiftly paid and hustled her outside. "Talking like that can get you in a lot of trouble, you know that?"

"Good." She gave him a mischievous grin. "Because, for the first time in a very long time, I'm really looking forward to a lot of trouble."

He looked at her and asked, "Are you sure?"

"Of course I'm sure," she replied, with a wave of her hand. "I'm an adult. Don't you dare insult me by making it sound like I don't know my own mind."

"I would never do that," he teased, "but I wasn't even planning on bringing it up this soon."

"No, I figured you'd go all noble and give me time. But you don't mind, do you?"

"God no, not at all," he said. "I just really hope that you don't change your mind before we get back to the hotel."

"Well, assuming we get back to the hotel without any trouble, without anybody else attacking us or preying on us or otherwise making it impossible for me to enjoy my future," she stated, "I have no intention of changing my mind."

And, with that, before she even realized it, they were already back at the hotel.

"How did you make that happen so fast?"

"Incentive," he said immediately.

She burst out laughing and soon found herself inside the room with him, slamming the door shut behind them.

He walked closer with a look in his eye that said she was in for a ride that would change her life.

She opened up her arms. "You know what? I've seen that dangerous look in your eyes so many times but never directed at me."

"The only way it'll ever be directed at you"—he lowered his voice into a deep dark growl—"is if you say things like you just did at the restaurant." Stepping forward, he opened his arms and wrapped her up in them.

"Good," she replied. "I hope to do that more than a few

times in the next few weeks."

"How about a lifetime?" he muttered, as he lowered his head.

"Works for me," she whispered. "God, yes, it works for me."

He lowered his head and took her lips in a searing kiss that had her heart slamming against her chest and made her knees weak. When he finally lifted his head, she stared at him in shock.

"My God," she whispered, "that lethal look is only part of your charm."

He burst out laughing, lifted her up, and carried her to the bed. "Enough talking. We have some serious time to make up for."

And, with that, he lowered his head and kissed her again. When he lifted his head the second time, her pants were being stripped from her legs and her blouse was open and her bra unclipped in the front.

She stared down at her body, now open to his gaze, and whispered, "You're more than lethal. I've never felt like this before." Sitting up, she quickly stripped off her bra and blouse, then stretched back out again with just her panties on. He looked down at them and swallowed hard. She waved her hand. "Oh no, you don't," she said. "You are wearing way too much."

He laughed, and, while she watched, he quickly divested himself of every stitch of clothing on his body. When he stood before her, proudly muscled and fully erect, she immediately bounded to her knees and stared. "Good God." Her gaze went to the scars on his chest and his abdomen.

He shrugged. "Do they bother you?"

"Only that you were hurt"—her gaze rose to his—

"obviously badly hurt."

"I recovered." He smiled. "It's all good." And then he wouldn't let her talk because she was flat on her back with his heated skin pressing her down.

And every inch of her came alive.

"Hatch," she whispered, and then she couldn't whisper at all, as his tongue trailed across her skin, over her ribs, down to her hip bones and her belly, then farther down to her knees. She laughed. She giggled. She cried, all while twisting under his ministrations, until she finally couldn't stand it anymore. "Dear God, don't torment me another second."

He slowly slid back up toward her face and whispered, "I really wouldn't want to make you suffer."

"No suffering." She pulled at him until he was on top of her. She split her legs wide and wrapped her long legs around his hips and whispered, "Now."

"Are you sure?" he asked, resting his weight on his elbows, as he gently dropped a kiss on her chin, on her nose, and across her cheeks.

She reached her arms up around his neck, pulled him down, and kissed him with all the passion she held deep inside, and, when she could, she whispered, "Yes, I'm sure."

And he slid inside, so deep that her breath caught deeper in her throat, and she arched up beneath him.

"Are you okay?" he asked, his voice gritty.

"Never better," she whispered. "Now move, dammit, move."

With a burst of laughter, he started to move deep inside her, the rhythm catching her up, harder and faster, until she couldn't do anything but cry out underneath the motion that rocked her to the core. When she finally exploded beneath him, she dimly heard him in the background, but she was so caught up in her own tidal wave of emotions that his own release barely registered.

Soon he crashed beside her, careful to keep his weight off her, and, when he reached across and stroked her cheek, he whispered, "All good?"

She had tears streaming down her cheeks. She wrapped her arms around him and curled up against him. "Dear God, yes," she murmured. "As a celebration of life over all that death," she explained, "it was absolutely perfect."

He held her close. "Sleep now. You need the rest."

She nodded. "But don't let me sleep too long."

"Why not?" he whispered.

"Because I want to enjoy this night as much as I can," she replied, "so wake me up … soon." And, with that, she closed her eyes.

When he woke up the next time, she opened her arms to him, to enjoy themselves again, then fell asleep when they were done. He awakened her several more times in the night. When she woke in the morning, it was her turn to wake him. When he finally rolled over, and they were sated yet again, he whispered, "You can wake me anytime you want."

She smiled. "Maybe, … but right now I am going back to sleep again." With that, she curled up and closed her eyes. But a smile was on her face, and she knew that her life would just get better from here on out.

EPILOGUE

C ORBIN WALLACE ENTERED his hotel room, worn out and ready for some rest.

He read the message from Hatch on his phone, telling Corbin to stay on his side of the adjoining rooms, and he laughed out loud. "Well, Hatch, you called it, and this one's all yours," he said, "but, dammit, I want the next one." With all the pressure of the last few days now resolved, he crashed himself and slept through the night. When he got up the next morning, he found more messages from Jonas, and Corbin knew that the next few days would be crazy busy.

He saw Millie and Hatch a couple times, but they were clearly in a world of their own, and Corbin was so happy for them. By the time he was done with MI6 and had a chance to catch up with the happy couple, Corbin looked over at Hatch and asked, "So, will you stay here for now?"

"Yeah, I will," he confirmed. "How are you doing? Is your arm okay?"

"Yeah, the bullet went a little deeper than I realized, but I'm good. Just worn out, but a few days of rest will be good for me."

"Well, hopefully that is something you get," Hatch noted, "but, as usual, there are never any guarantees."

"I know. Apparently the next job is just around the corner."

"It is," Hatch confirmed. "Sounds like I'll be your handler."

Corbin smiled. "And I presume you'll be handling it from here?"

"Absolutely, since I have a reason to stay close." He watched as Millie neared, and when he held out his hand, Millie immediately grabbed on to it and smiled back.

"I'll help MI6 go through all the contents of the warehouse," she said, looking over at Corbin. "I suspect it'll take a few weeks."

He laughed. "Are you kidding? That'll take a few months." But he said to Hatch, "Just give me a couple days to recuperate, if you can."

"If I can," he said. "And then we'll figure out where you're going."

"Maybe nowhere," Corbin suggested. "Maybe it'll be nice and calm, and we'll just stay here in England."

"Hey, it's possible," Hatch admitted, "and I'm not against that at all."

"Good," Corbin murmured. "Give me a couple days, and then we'll talk."

But it wasn't a couple days; it was only a day and a half. Just as Corbin stepped out of the shower, his phone rang.

When he answered, Hatch asked, "Are you ready?"

"Yeah, sure I am. Where am I going?"

"Scotland," he replied.

"Scotland, *huh.* Well, that's not too far from here. What's up?"

"We're not exactly sure yet, but a woman and two children have been kidnapped. They've been gone for two weeks, and now another woman with two children were kidnapped as well."

"I'm sure Scotland Yard doesn't want me there."

"Maybe not, but, as of now, there has been a third woman taken."

"Well, *great*," he noted. "Does she have kids too?"

"No," Hatch replied. "No kids at all. But she *is* pregnant."

"How on earth is this a good deal, … even for a kidnapper?"

"It isn't, and the body of the first mother just showed up, and unfortunately the kids are missing."

"Shit," Corbin said, his heart sinking. "You know how I feel about kids."

"I know, and, if you want to pass on this one, just tell me."

"No, I'm not passing on nothing," he snapped. "I'll go in there and get that bastard. I can't stand any rat bastard who preys on kids. I'll take him down. Don't you worry."

"Oh, I believe you will," Hatch said. "Say hi to Nellie for me."

"Who is Nellie?" Corbin asked suspiciously.

"The niece of Scotland's Secretary of State. She's the latest pregnant woman who's gone missing."

"And do you know her?" Corbin couldn't understand how such a connection could have come about.

"Nope," he replied. "But obviously it's your turn, so chances are she'll become a good friend during this investigation. In which case I'll say hi in advance."

Corbin laughed. "Oh, Jesus, that's all I need. Well, I'll believe you when I see it. You look after Millie while I'm gone now."

"Count on it," Hatch said. "And you watch your back. I don't like that I won't be there to watch it for you."

And, with that, Corbin hung up and turned to pack. He knew this op would be hard, given the kids element. It also needed to go down fast, and he needed to do it right. But, as always, he was ready.

"Well, Nellie, for better or for worse, here I come."

This concludes Book 16 of The Mavericks: Hatch.

Read about Corbin: The Mavericks, Book 17

Corbin: Maverick (Book #17)

What happens when the very men—trained to make the hard decisions—come up against the rules and regulations that hold them back from doing what needs to be done? They either stay and work within the constraints given to them or they walk away. Only now, for a select few, they have another option:

The Mavericks. A covert black ops team that steps up and break all the rules … but gets the job done.

Welcome to a new military romance series by *USA Today* best-selling author Dale Mayer. A series where you meet new friends and just might get to meet old ones too in this raw and compelling look at the men who keep us safe every day from the darkness where they operate—and live—in the shadows … until someone special helps them step into the light.

Corbin is tracking a cabinet minister's pregnant daughter, who'd been snatched off the streets several days ago. The incident followed several other missing women's cases, except those women already had given birth, and their children were also kidnapped at the same time. Then the body of one of the mothers is found …

Nellie would do anything to save her unborn child, but finding herself a prisoner was never something she expected to happen. When one of her guards grills her over an image of someone asking questions about her, she realizes she isn't as alone as she'd assumed. Now if only a rescue could be mounted before any others die …

A rescue is one thing, but getting to the bottom of this nightmare becomes even more urgent, as the kidnapper refuses to give up on Nellie's unborn child and the big payoff if he succeeds …

Find book 17 here!
To find out more visit Dale Mayer's website.
https://geni.us/DMCorbinUniversal

Author's Note

Thank you for reading Hatch: The Mavericks, Book 16! If you enjoyed the book, please take a moment and leave a short review.

Dear reader,

I love to hear from readers, and you can contact me at my website: www.dalemayer.com or at my Facebook author page. To be informed of new releases and special offers, sign up for my newsletter or follow me on BookBub. And if you are interested in joining Dale Mayer's Reader Group, here is the Facebook sign up page.
http://geni.us/DaleMayerFBGroup

Cheers,
Dale Mayer

About the Author

Dale Mayer is a *USA Today* best-selling author, best known for her SEALs military romances, her Psychic Visions series, and her Lovely Lethal Garden cozy series. Her contemporary romances are raw and full of passion and emotion (Broken But … Mending, Hathaway House series). Her thrillers will keep you guessing (Kate Morgan, By Death series), and her romantic comedies will keep you giggling (*It's a Dog's Life*, a stand-alone novella; and the Broken Protocols series, starring Charming Marvin, the cat).

Dale honors the stories that come to her—and some of them are crazy, break all the rules and cross multiple genres!

To go with her fiction, she also writes nonfiction in many different fields, with books available on résumé writing, companion gardening, and the US mortgage system. All her books are available in print and ebook format.

Connect with Dale Mayer Online

Dale's Website – www.dalemayer.com

Twitter – @DaleMayer

Facebook Page – geni.us/DaleMayerFBFanPage

Facebook Group – geni.us/DaleMayerFBGroup

BookBub – geni.us/DaleMayerBookbub

Instagram – geni.us/DaleMayerInstagram

Goodreads – geni.us/DaleMayerGoodreads

Newsletter – geni.us/DaleNews

Also by Dale Mayer

Published Adult Books:

Bullard's Battle
Ryland's Reach, Book 1
Cain's Cross, Book 2
Eton's Escape, Book 3
Garret's Gambit, Book 4
Kano's Keep, Book 5
Fallon's Flaw, Book 6
Quinn's Quest, Book 7
Bullard's Beauty, Book 8
Bullard's Best, Book 9

Terkel's Team
Damon's Deal, Book 1

Kate Morgan
Simon Says… Hide, Book 1
Simon Says… Jump, Book 2
Simon Says… Ride, Book 3
Simon Says… Scream, Book 4

Hathaway House
Aaron, Book 1
Brock, Book 2
Cole, Book 3
Denton, Book 4

Elliot, Book 5
Finn, Book 6
Gregory, Book 7
Heath, Book 8
Iain, Book 9
Jaden, Book 10
Keith, Book 11
Lance, Book 12
Melissa, Book 13
Nash, Book 14
Owen, Book 15
Percy, Book 16
Hathaway House, Books 1–3
Hathaway House, Books 4–6
Hathaway House, Books 7–9

The K9 Files

Ethan, Book 1
Pierce, Book 2
Zane, Book 3
Blaze, Book 4
Lucas, Book 5
Parker, Book 6
Carter, Book 7
Weston, Book 8
Greyson, Book 9
Rowan, Book 10
Caleb, Book 11
Kurt, Book 12
Tucker, Book 13
Harley, Book 14
Kyron, Book 15

The K9 Files, Books 1–2
The K9 Files, Books 3–4
The K9 Files, Books 5–6
The K9 Files, Books 7–8
The K9 Files, Books 9–10
The K9 Files, Books 11–12

Lovely Lethal Gardens
Arsenic in the Azaleas, Book 1
Bones in the Begonias, Book 2
Corpse in the Carnations, Book 3
Daggers in the Dahlias, Book 4
Evidence in the Echinacea, Book 5
Footprints in the Ferns, Book 6
Gun in the Gardenias, Book 7
Handcuffs in the Heather, Book 8
Ice Pick in the Ivy, Book 9
Jewels in the Juniper, Book 10
Killer in the Kiwis, Book 11
Lifeless in the Lilies, Book 12
Murder in the Marigolds, Book 13
Nabbed in the Nasturtiums, Book 14
Offed in the Orchids, Book 15
Poison in the Pansies, Book 16
Lovely Lethal Gardens, Books 1–2
Lovely Lethal Gardens, Books 3–4
Lovely Lethal Gardens, Books 5–6
Lovely Lethal Gardens, Books 7–8
Lovely Lethal Gardens, Books 9–10

Psychic Vision Series
Tuesday's Child
Hide 'n Go Seek

Maddy's Floor
Garden of Sorrow
Knock Knock…
Rare Find
Eyes to the Soul
Now You See Her
Shattered
Into the Abyss
Seeds of Malice
Eye of the Falcon
Itsy-Bitsy Spider
Unmasked
Deep Beneath
From the Ashes
Stroke of Death
Ice Maiden
Snap, Crackle…
What If…
Talking Bones
Psychic Visions Books 1–3
Psychic Visions Books 4–6
Psychic Visions Books 7–9

By Death Series
Touched by Death
Haunted by Death
Chilled by Death
By Death Books 1–3

Broken Protocols – Romantic Comedy Series
Cat's Meow
Cat's Pajamas
Cat's Cradle

Cat's Claus

Broken Protocols 1-4

Broken and... Mending

Skin

Scars

Scales (of Justice)

Broken but... Mending 1-3

Glory

Genesis

Tori

Celeste

Glory Trilogy

Biker Blues

Morgan: Biker Blues, Volume 1

Cash: Biker Blues, Volume 2

SEALs of Honor

Mason: SEALs of Honor, Book 1

Hawk: SEALs of Honor, Book 2

Dane: SEALs of Honor, Book 3

Swede: SEALs of Honor, Book 4

Shadow: SEALs of Honor, Book 5

Cooper: SEALs of Honor, Book 6

Markus: SEALs of Honor, Book 7

Evan: SEALs of Honor, Book 8

Mason's Wish: SEALs of Honor, Book 9

Chase: SEALs of Honor, Book 10

Brett: SEALs of Honor, Book 11

Devlin: SEALs of Honor, Book 12

Easton: SEALs of Honor, Book 13

Ryder: SEALs of Honor, Book 14
Macklin: SEALs of Honor, Book 15
Corey: SEALs of Honor, Book 16
Warrick: SEALs of Honor, Book 17
Tanner: SEALs of Honor, Book 18
Jackson: SEALs of Honor, Book 19
Kanen: SEALs of Honor, Book 20
Nelson: SEALs of Honor, Book 21
Taylor: SEALs of Honor, Book 22
Colton: SEALs of Honor, Book 23
Troy: SEALs of Honor, Book 24
Axel: SEALs of Honor, Book 25
Baylor: SEALs of Honor, Book 26
Hudson: SEALs of Honor, Book 27
Lachlan: SEALs of Honor, Book 28
SEALs of Honor, Books 1–3
SEALs of Honor, Books 4–6
SEALs of Honor, Books 7–10
SEALs of Honor, Books 11–13
SEALs of Honor, Books 14–16
SEALs of Honor, Books 17–19
SEALs of Honor, Books 20–22
SEALs of Honor, Books 23–25

Heroes for Hire

Levi's Legend: Heroes for Hire, Book 1
Stone's Surrender: Heroes for Hire, Book 2
Merk's Mistake: Heroes for Hire, Book 3
Rhodes's Reward: Heroes for Hire, Book 4
Flynn's Firecracker: Heroes for Hire, Book 5
Logan's Light: Heroes for Hire, Book 6
Harrison's Heart: Heroes for Hire, Book 7

SEALs of Steel

Talon: SEALs of Steel, Book 4
Laszlo: SEALs of Steel, Book 5
Geir: SEALs of Steel, Book 6
Jager: SEALs of Steel, Book 7
The Final Reveal: SEALs of Steel, Book 8
SEALs of Steel, Books 1–4
SEALs of Steel, Books 5–8
SEALs of Steel, Books 1–8

The Mavericks

Kerrick, Book 1
Griffin, Book 2
Jax, Book 3
Beau, Book 4
Asher, Book 5
Ryker, Book 6
Miles, Book 7
Nico, Book 8
Keane, Book 9
Lennox, Book 10
Gavin, Book 11
Shane, Book 12
Diesel, Book 13
Jerricho, Book 14
Killian, Book 15
Hatch, Book 16
Corbin, Book 17
The Mavericks, Books 1–2
The Mavericks, Books 3–4
The Mavericks, Books 5–6
The Mavericks, Books 7–8
The Mavericks, Books 9–10

The Mavericks, Books 11–12

Collections
Dare to Be You…
Dare to Love…
Dare to be Strong…
RomanceX3

Standalone Novellas
It's a Dog's Life
Riana's Revenge
Second Chances

Published Young Adult Books:

Family Blood Ties Series
Vampire in Denial
Vampire in Distress
Vampire in Design
Vampire in Deceit
Vampire in Defiance
Vampire in Conflict
Vampire in Chaos
Vampire in Crisis
Vampire in Control
Vampire in Charge
Family Blood Ties Set 1–3
Family Blood Ties Set 1–5
Family Blood Ties Set 4–6
Family Blood Ties Set 7–9
Sian's Solution, A Family Blood Ties Series Prequel
    Novelette

Design series
Dangerous Designs
Deadly Designs
Darkest Designs
Design Series Trilogy

Standalone
In Cassie's Corner
Gem Stone (a Gemma Stone Mystery)
Time Thieves

Published Non-Fiction Books:

Career Essentials
Career Essentials: The Résumé
Career Essentials: The Cover Letter
Career Essentials: The Interview
Career Essentials: 3 in 1